COMING
ABOUT

The Roger Vaughan Library

COMING ABOUT

A Novel

BY ROGER VAUGHAN

Choptank Word Bank

The Roger Vaughan Library

Published by Choptank Word Bank
Bachelor's Point, Oxford, Maryland
www.choptankwordbank.com

ISBN 978-1-7333135-4-4
Library of Congress Control Number: 2021912043

Cover Photograph: Carlo Borlinghi

Cover and Interior Design: Joseph Daniel
www.storyartsmedia.com

POD Edition
Printed in the United States

For Kippy

Table of Contents

I

NEAR MISS

The video re-ran several times a year in Andy's dreams. It was always the same, down to the last detail, and it never failed to leave him with a hollow, perplexed feeling. If the conditions were right it could play in broad daylight, as it did this particular July afternoon, induced by the monotony of riding the rail of his father's boat. *Worthy*, a competitive fifty-footer, was sailing upwind in a vacillating but strong flow of warm breeze, the hull rising and falling with a slow, roller-coaster rhythm through the big ground swells off Newport, Rhode Island. Such conditions provoked either seasickness or ennui. Andy and the rest of the crew were facing westward into a late-afternoon sun that had dropped out of the high overcast and was turning the water's surface into a million sparkling, hypnotic diamonds. The soft, white-noise wash of water against the hull as the boat slid down the backsides of the broad swells helped bring on Andy's reverie. His head drooped against the lifelines. His eyes closed.

It was ten years ago. Andy and his friend Robby were fourteen, goofing on their mountain bikes at the 57th Street entrance to Manhattan's Central Park, waiting for Mitchell Thomas, Andy's father. And there came the great man, on cue, promptly at six thirty p.m., dapper as hell on his spotless, dark-green Raleigh three-speed he'd special-ordered from England, the one with the enclosed metal chain guard, chromed brake rods, narrow fenders pinstriped in gold, and natty wicker basket. His Mark Cross briefcase with his Brooks Brothers suit jacket neatly folded on top were strapped to the rear carrier. His neck-tie bearing the burgee of the New York Yacht Club had been flipped over his shoulder by the headwind.

Every time he saw Mitchell this way Andy felt as if he were watching one of those TV commercials where a period person was presented in black and white against a contemporary scene in color. Not a hair on Mitchell's head as much as fluttered in the breeze. Mitchell may as well have been a paid actor for all the paternal connection he inspired in Andy at these times.

Mitchell didn't stop, didn't speak, just nodded to the boys with his habitual, all-purpose executive grin, and rode into the park. The boys fell in behind him like dogs at heel. Robby peeled off at 72nd Street, heading for his family's apartment on the East Side. Andy got distracted by irre-sistible, off-path opportunities, skidding through some soft new landscaping, jumping off a wall, and crashing through a hedge and nearly running over a couple entwined behind it until he heard Mitchell's angry shout. He turned his bike sharply and quickly caught up to his father.

Mitchell seemed more upset than usual about Andy fooling around on his daily ride home. Something had to be bugging him. What a jerk, his father. How could this man even be his father? "Keep up," Mitchell warned in that terse way of his. Keep up. Yeah, right. Hey Mr. Movie Guy on your stupid three-speed, *you* keep up! Andy pulled a wheelie and took off, leaving his father shouting after him. There would be hell to pay, but his mother would intervene, as usual. Even at fourteen, Andy understood that Mitchell didn't dare mess with his mom. It was her company, her money. Andy would speed around the pedestrian tunnel up ahead and lie in wait for his father, give him a scare. The predator in the park.

Tucked behind a big tree, Andy waited. But Mitchell didn't come out of the tunnel. Maybe he'd taken a different route? Not Mitchell. Andy thought he heard voices; it sounded like an argument but it was hard to be sure against the dull jungle roar of the city that invaded the park. Then he did hear someone yell. Twice. It was Mitchell's voice, for sure, only he couldn't make out the word. It did sound like one word, repeated. But the gunshot, amplified by the tunnel, was unmistakable. It sent a chill up Andy's spine, momentarily freezing him to the big oak tree. Two guys emerged from the tunnel on the run, split up, and disappeared into the gathering dusk. Andy waited, fear constricting his chest. He jumped when a squirrel scampered away above him. It took all his will to leave the protection of the old oak, and not to pedal full speed toward the West Side and home. He coasted cautiously down the slight incline and into the tunnel.

Mitchell was on his knees in the semi-darkness, the precious Raleigh down at a bad angle beside him. He was clutching his right forearm. When he looked up, his face was drawn with pain and shock. When he saw Andy, the pain mixed with rage. Andy was fixed on the blood seeping between Mitchell's fingers, slick and dark. Andy's throat was dry. He felt sick.

Mitchell struggled to his feet, sputtering incoherently. Andy's rising nausea combined with his fear to freeze him in place. His feet felt glued to the damp concrete of the tunnel floor. He watched his father struggle to regain his feet and stagger toward him, maniacal in his disarray, howling with force that spewed saliva. Andy felt it on his face. "You . . . bastard!" Mitchell screamed at him, the veins in his neck like ropes. The word was expelled with such power that it blew past Mitchell's vocal chords as part screech. "You BASTARD!" Mitchell half turned away only to snap back, his left hand releasing the fresh wound just long enough to smack Andy on the side of his head with a savage growl and all the strength he could muster.

Still astride his bike, Andy went down, little points of light twinkling behind his eyes. He hadn't seen the hand that felled him, he had been so intently focused on the blood-soaked shirtsleeve covering where the bullet had entered. Luckily for Andy, Mitchell's wild swing had only partially connected, but it had left blood on his face. His father's blood.

Even as he went down and before normal vision returned Andy was reflexively scrabbling away on hands and knees, dragging his bike, somehow getting it upright, running, jumping on one pedal and pushing hard, swinging into the saddle, bouncing once off the rough stone wall of the tunnel, pedaling with all he had along the familiar paths, his breath choked by sobs; hearing the crash, but never seeing the taxi that swerved into a parked car to miss him as he sprinted blindly out of the park onto Central Park West.

"Tacking."

Mitchell's voice brought Andy back with a start. The crewmen on either side of him chuckled. "Hey, jus' grabbin' a siesta," one of them cracked as they jackknifed their legs in and scampered across the deck to the new high side as the boat changed tacks.

Andy had become a scruffy twenty-four-year-old. He was twenty pounds overweight with a habitually unkempt shock of thick dark hair. His clothes looked slept-in. He looked like a person with a habitual hangover. That was often the case. Mitchell's crew was a spit-and-polish lot. They made the midshipmen aboard the Naval Academy boats look slightly tarnished. Andy would have stood out in any crowd. On this boat, he was a sore thumb.

Worthy was on the new tack for twenty minutes. But they were closing the layline, that imaginary path that would take them to the finish line on the other tack. Close also was *Fetching*, their main rival in this regatta. The two boats had been practically match racing all weekend. They'd split tacks as they'd entered the passage marked by Brenton Light. *Fetching* had chosen the east side, a move that would put it on starboard tack with right-of-way when they came together before the finish line. Whoever won that cross would take the race and the regatta. As *Worthy* tacked again, Andy heard the bowman announce that *Fetching* was also tacking.

Andy was the jib trimmer on the new tack. He took a third turn on the big winch drum and hauled hard and fast on the sheet. Given his slack look, his proficiency was surprising. "Trim," he said quietly to the man on the coffee-grinder handles. "Stop." Andy watched the jib, watched the speedo on the mast climbing quickly toward the optimum. "Three clicks, one more, stop."

"Get it right," Mitchell said from the wheel.

"It is."

"It better be."

Crewmen on the rail exchanged looks while Andy quietly simmered. Michell never stopped ragging Andy. The great Mitchell Thomas, hail fellow, captain of industry, excellent sailor. As the twentieth century drew to a close, he was one of the few amateurs who still steered his own boat and held his own in a fleet full of professionals. Good old Mitch. Good old son of a bitch was Andy's version. Those who fawned over him should have to live just one day with him. They crewed for him for only one reason: he frequently won.

"Have we got them?"

Mitchell was addressing Andy, the only one on the lee side, the one with the best view of *Fetching*. The big genoa effectively blocked the view for the rest. For a moment, Mitchell silently cursed Rummans, his sailmaker and deck boss, for having assigned Andy to trim on the burdened port tack. Then he remembered. Jonesy, the regular port trimmer, had taken ill. Couldn't make it. Better to have Andy there than some untested new guy. That was the theory anyway.

"No problem."

"Get that weight outboard." Mitchell addressed the crew in terse tones. "Let's have it quiet."

Intensity permeated the deck like heavy oil. There was no chatter from the railbirds. The mains'l trimmer's eyes flicked from sail to instruments to sail. He took one click on the traveler, pulling the boom to windward maybe an inch. In the lulls, Andy eased the jib sheet an inch, called for a click or two of trim in the puffs.

"How we doing?" Mitchell stood erect, his face locked in concentration.

Andy said, "No problem."

Sitting furthest forward on the rail, the bowman stretched himself forward to grab a quick look through the clear plastic window sewn into the genoa. "Close," he muttered to no one in particular.

Andy heard him. "No problem."

"By how much?" Mitchell demanded.

"Enough."

Conley, the tactician, interrupted the edgy father-son exchange. "Are we good? If not we'll tack early, lee-bow them, hope to give them some bad air, maybe pick up a header we can tack on. Better to cross them and then tack, pin them outside until we can lay the finish line."

"We're good." Andy sounded confident.

Head down, the bowman stared into the bow wave under his feet, shook his head, started to speak, then decided to stay out of it. But he could feel it coming. It wouldn't be the first time Andy and the old man had gotten it on.

"Starboard!"

The warning hail came from *Fetching*. The right-of-way boat always made a fuss trying to rattle the confidence of the crew hoping to cross. Making a close cross from the burdened position took a lot of cool, a lot of guts, and a keen eye. It was like running a stop sign when you knew a car was coming. The helmsman had to steer perfectly under pressure, maintaining the optimum combination of boat speed and heading. Large sailboats don't travel very fast, but they carry great momentum. For boats the size of *Worthy* and *Fetching*, their combined weight was around 80,000 pounds — coming together at a closing speed of roughly twenty knots (twenty-three miles per hour) would be like two lightly loaded eighteen-wheelers colliding head-on when each was moving faster than ten miles an hour. Boats have no brakes. And the water they are moving through is an unstable platform. Misjudge a close cross, and the havoc of a collision was a good possibility. Damage could be extensive. The mast could come down. There could be serious injuries. The person making the call had to be very good, very confident in himself and in his helmsman. And vice versa.

A few moments passed. The only sounds were the slice of the cutwater, and the eddies of water separating from the polished hull with a steady fizz.

"Starboard!" The hail was closer. This time there was more than a touch of frenzy in the call. And there were other voices chiming in, a sure sign that anxiety was becoming a factor aboard *Fetching*.

"Better tack!" *Worthy's* bowman found his voice.

"Starboard! Hey! Starboardgoddammit! . . . STAR-BOARD . . . HEY!!"

Andy: "Tack, Mitchell. Tack! Tack *now!*"

"Don't you tell me . . . Christ! . . . Tacking!" Cursing a blue streak, Mitchell Thomas drove the wheel down hard as he caught sight of *Fetching* coming into his path like a train, spinning *Worthy* on a dime to avoid the impending collision. The violent turn drastically reduced the boat's forward motion. The crew sensed the crisis coming, and still used up valuable seconds getting off the rail and scrambling up the deck that was now tilted against them. Andy had to let the jib sheet run before the new trimmer was ready. It took precious seconds to overhaul the loose sheet and get the big jib in on the new tack. *Worthy* had avoided a collision, but it was a racing disaster.

Fetching passed by very close at full tilt, the wash of the hull frighteningly loud. *Fetching's* skipper, Alistair Koonce, took a certain amount of pleasure cutting it as close as he dared, but he smartly eased his helm toward the wind five degrees to make sure he avoided *Worthy*, and so his mast would straighten up a bit and avoid slamming into *Worthy's* now nearly upright rig. The sailors on both boats avoided one another's eyes. No one on either boat said a word, except the outraged Mitchell Thomas, who kept up a vicious string of abuse directed at Andy, whose face remained impassive.

Koonce, a savvy New Zealand professional at the top of his game, let the hint of a smile cross his lips at the stream of invective coming from *Worthy*.

"Sounds like someone's upset," he said quietly. His

crew, wound tight from the near miss, convulsed with laughter.

Koonce tacked for the finish line. With *Worthy* now tucked four boat-lengths behind them, and the finish less than a mile ahead, the race was over. Koonce and crew were winners, but they tended to business, watched the trim, tidied up lines and got ready to cross the line in style. Koonce gave the wheel to Rufus Samuels, the owner. Judd, *Fetching*'s tactician, a regular with Koonce, shook his head as Koonce sat down beside him.

"Why's he do it? Why's he take the kid? Why's the kid go?"

Koonce shrugged. The race was history. He was already thinking about a beer, and other business.

"I know Deedee, Mrs. Thomas, Deedee Moss," Rufus Samuels offered from behind the wheel. "She likes it that Andy sails on the boat. She insists, in fact. And since she is the majority stockholder in the company, well, let's just say Mitchell has always been a realist." Samuels paused. He chuckled, happily patted the wheel. "Our good luck. I thought they might have crossed us back there."

II

GAFFE

Isha Mowbry let out a shriek as Andy drifted his shiny new Porsche Carrera G50 through the fieldstone gateposts that marked the entrance to Harbour Court, the New York Yacht Club's Newport station. The imposing limestone mansion rose majestically above the trees in the twilight. It had been built in 1906 for John Nicholas Brown, whose ancestors had amassed several fortunes in shipping during the days of the notorious Triangle Trade. Rum from New England had been shipped to West Africa for slaves who were shipped to the Caribbean to cut cane and process sugar that was sent to New England. How fitting, Andy often thought, that this mansion would become the headquarters for the New York Yacht Club's latter-day captains of industry, if not ships.

He downshifted, the tires spraying gravel as the Porsche charged up the gentle hill to the parking lot, skidding to a stop on the grass after knocking over a recently planted sapling. One of the assistant managers glowered at Andy from the steps of the club. "Hey," Andy yelled at the man, "send me a bill. Better yet, send Mitchell a bill."

Laughing, he grabbed the drink that was nestled in his crotch, got out of the car, walked around the back, and opened the door for Isha. Manners came naturally to Andy, even when he was half looped. Manners, in this case, that had their reward. The low-slung Porsche was excellent for looking down the fronts of female passengers' dresses. When the passenger was Isha, it didn't get any better. She rarely wore underwear, a fact her choice of clothing always advertised. Andy swore Isha would go topless through life if she could get away with it, especially since she'd had the implants. Gilded lilies. The best Andy's money could buy. And there they were, thank you Jesus. As she swung her long, bronzed legs out of the car and bent to get up, he could see down to her waist.

Isha was a sight, a trophy babe par excellence. Her face was captivating with the flashing eyes that were impossibly round, the shapely lips so expressive, the silky tone of her skin, the blond-streaked hair in studied disarray. This day in her yellow sundress that moved elegantly in the breeze, topped by the matching summer straw hat with long ribbons, she could stop traffic. It wasn't just a dress, it was a costume. The hat was an excellent addition. Clutching it in the wind gave Isha a whole range of new moves. And when the right men were downwind, letting it blow off always caused a scramble. If she bent to pick it up, the result was even better. Andy was fond of saying if Helen of Troy's face launched a thousand ships, Isha's tits would have sunk them. The members' wives deplored her, but that simply added spice to Isha's act.

Andy and Isha hustled through the club to the waterside. Bursts of applause indicated that the prize-giving was in progress. As luck would have it, they arrived just in time to catch the end of the commodore's announcement that Mitchell Thomas had taken second overall: " . . . and a marvelous competitor, a man who's been in the silver year after year for longer than I care to remember. The boats keep changing, technology makes the competition increasingly tougher, and the pros give us fits, but Mitchell Thomas keeps that amateur flag flying for all of us, God love him . . . "

Grabbing a couple hot hors d'oeuvres from a tray passed by a waiter in a starched white jacket, Andy cringed. Ease up, Commodore Critchfield. What a joke. Critchfield looked like what he was, a Fortune 500 CEO. He was tall, flat-faced, and had a voice with no affect. A colorless, odorless numbers man of the new millennium who sailed the same way he ran his company: to compete without joy. He never took his boat off the mooring if the race committee wasn't on station, unless it was to test a new sail. Nice evening cruise with the family? Forget it, unless it was for media coverage. Listen to this freaking robot. He could have been addressing a stockholder meeting. Or doing a eulogy for a loyal company officer.

The applause was enthusiastic as Mitchell made his way through the crowd to the trophy table, doing his best humble-guy routine with that smile pasted in place. As

Mitchell raised his glittering cup for all to admire, Andy felt a tug on his arm. It was Admiral Barnes, the oldest member of the Club. He was well into his nineties and still afloat. He seemed even smaller now than when Andy had last seen him six months ago. The shrinking syndrome of old age. Andy wondered if you lived to be two or three hundred years old you would end up two feet tall. It made sense. Eventually you would disappear altogether.

"Hell of a man, your father," Barnes said, his weight on Andy's arm like an anchor. His breath was rank.

"Yes sir." Andy wanted to bolt. He hated coming to the Club. Isha had insisted. "Hell of a sailor," Barnes said.

"Yes sir," Andy said, turning away from a blast of Barnes's pungent vapors.

"Your mother was even better."

Andy's head snapped back at Barnes's remark. He looked hard at the old man, who was grinning at him, showing square yellow teeth beneath the steely little eyes that were boring in, measuring the effect of his last salvo. Andy had heard his mother was a hot sailor as a young girl, but no one ever spoke about it. She wouldn't talk about it, as if it were something to be ashamed of. He never could understand. But he'd let it go. Now here was Barnes . . .

"What happened out there today?" Barnes had commanded a submarine in World War II, sunk a bunch of ships, been sunk once himself, and had decorations and citations enough to paper the walls of his study. He'd ended up at the Pentagon. He still had that icy-command presence. Even at ninety-odd, Barnes was a little scary to Andy. After watching your first torpedo find its mark, sending several hundred humans to agonizing deaths in flaming, shark-infested waters, there must be no turning back. Andy had the instant feeling that Barnes knew damn well what had happened out there. The old man's grin had been replaced by thin-lipped authority. Court-martial time.

"Bad wind shift at the last minute," Andy mumbled, quite off balance.

Barnes stared at Andy in a way that was unsettling. Then his face softened. He pulled Andy even closer, patted the young man's arm. "Too bad." This was feeling much too personal. Barnes continued: "Your father would have won it," he said softly. Having this gruff old geezer go suddenly compassionate on him was a curveball. He was set up to deal with Admiral Barnes, the hunter-killer. Grandpa Barnes threw him for a loop. The old man started to say something else.

"Admiral Barnes!" Isha had whirled around Andy, bending to greet the old man as if he were a four-year-old. Barnes ignored the display of Isha's charms, never taking his eyes off Andy. "What a pleasure to see you again," Isha crooned. "Let's go find a seat and have a talk." Isha took Barnes's arm. The old man didn't resist as Isha turned him away from Andy and the crowd toward a vacant umbrella table on the lawn. As Barnes's eyes left his, it felt like Velcro tearing. Isha tossed Andy a professional wink over her shoulder.

Andy raised his glass and found it empty. Old Barnes. Gettin' strange. Good time to get a drink before the presentation wrapped up and the bar got jammed. My father would have won it. What did that mean. Ha. Not today, Admiral, not today. Wonder what other nonsense he had in mind. Probably a few too many emergency dives for the old admiral. A few too many dives.

Dorothy Moss Thomas, known to everyone as Deedee, was having trouble buttering her roll. The butter pat from the iced, silver-plated serving dish was too firm, and it just wouldn't stay put. Deedee showed no sign of annoyance as she worked diligently with her knife. She seemed relaxed. Her posture was upright, and her face was pleasantly passive as usual, not betraying for a second whatever was occupying her mind. Her husband, Mitchell, in conversation with one of the sailors down the table about some technical aspect of *Worthy*'s rig, never missed a beat as he dabbed butter on a section of roll and casually placed it on his wife's plate. Without so much as a nod in Mitchell's direction, Mrs. Thomas abandoned her own roll project, picked up the buttered offering, and took a wee bite.

The dining room at Harbour Court was filled to capacity. Tables had been moved together to accommodate the Sunday-evening crew dinners. The dining room was large, airy, set back only a few dozen feet from the edge of the high, steep bluff of lush, mowed grass where the club was located. Several large windows provided a dazzling view of Newport Harbor and the town, with Goat Island beyond, and the big suspension bridge from Newport to Jamestown spanning the entrance to Mt. Hope Bay.

Mitchell Thomas presided over the *Worthy* table, a well-mannered party of twenty, counting wives and dates. At his left was his wife, Deedee to those who would be her friends, heiress to the Moss Optical fortune founded by her father. She was in her late fifties and looked much too old and frail for her age. One might have guessed she was in her mid-seventies. In part, it was the dated cut of her wardrobe. And she achieved a certain period dignity with her understated but priceless heirloom jewelry, her sparingly elegant use of cosmetics, and her old-fashioned permed hair that she had professionally maintained every week.

Those who had known Deedee longest couldn't recall her wearing her hair any other way. The only change was the gray cast that had arrived in the last year. No color rinses for Deedee Moss. She wouldn't hear of such a thing. The name "Deedee" didn't seem to fit this shy, weary-looking woman. It was one of those childhood nicknames that stuck.

She always made an appearance at the regatta gatherings, but kept to herself, said little. If her dinner companions felt obliged to engage her, as they dutifully did in turn, they would find her charming, but distant. She had her favorites among Mitchell's crew, and care was always taken to seat them near her. But even with the chosen few, Deedee would often drift off in mid-sentence, or lapse into long quiet periods of concentration on her meal. She knew sailing. That wasn't the problem. She could still talk tactics and sail shape. Both her father and grandfather had loved boats, and she had in fact been a savvy racer as a teenager. But Deedee seemed as miscast within this group as her son.

Andy sat with Isha at the other end of the table, as far from Mitchell as possible. While Mitchell maintained his skipper/owner posture, getting on with the crew like one of the guys, Andy got quietly drunker. There wasn't much else to do. Isha was flirting with a couple of crewmen sitting across the table who were barely able to control their drool reflexes. Nothing new there. She had gotten them going on the differences between men and women. Isha maintained that the only real difference was that women overcooked chicken. Andy watched the conversation do a slow burn down the table until Mitchell jumped in with his two cents, saying that women were definitely better with their hands, that's why there had been so many women welders during World War II after all, and now Isha was putting her moves on Mitchell. Andy got up and went to the bar for another drink.

When he returned, Alastair Koonce was standing at the head of the table, talking with Mitchell. This was an interesting development. Andy perked up. The conversation had the table's attention, especially that of Deedee, whose gaze was riveted on the handsome, bronzed New Zealander. He was tall and lanky, his face weather-beaten and his head aglow with a mass of tight blond curls. Andy hoped his mother wouldn't let her tongue hang out. He chuckled to himself. He'd missed the opening pleasantries. Now Koonce was launched into a round-the-world ocean-race rap. Someone must have asked him about his upcoming campaign for the 2000 race. Or maybe he'd just gotten into it. He was selling, after all, always on the lookout for sponsors. Alistair Koonce didn't have any small talk. Whenever you saw Koonce approaching, you got ready to do business.

Koonce knew how to work a table. First he played to Mitchell's crew, any one of whom would have sold out his mates for a chance to sail with this guy. Koonce had done three of the round-the-world races, winning one of them, a mighty accomplishment. It was 30,000 miles around the world over a nine-month period with half a dozen or more stopovers. When the race began in 1973, the boats had some degree of comfort. Real bunks, real galleys, and some skippers even took a case of wine along just to be civilized. But the races Koonce had done were anything but civilized. Most sailors wouldn't consider taking the modern boats on an overnight race, let alone a 30,000-mile odyssey. They were sixty-five feet long and they only weighed 30,000 pounds, half of which was in the keel. The ends of the boat were empty because it was bad (slow) to have any weight in the ends, so twelve crew lived in a thirty-five-foot space. There were no bunks, per se. Even the pipe berths of a few years ago had been discarded in the interest of saving weight. The off watch lined up on an eighteen-inch "shelf" formed into the hull, sleeping head-to-head, foot-to-foot. If the boat tacked, the sleepers awoke and switched to the high side. If the boat hit a wave and stopped, the off watch got compressed. The open head (toilet) was forward. And of course there was no seat. Got to save weight. The boats went so fast it was scary. They'd been clocked at over thirty knots. They were like race cars. You had to throttle them back in certain conditions to keep them from spinning out, self-destructing. The decks were flush, with nothing protecting the guys in the cockpit from the water fire-hosing off the bow with enough force to knock them senseless. Going round the world on one of these things was like climbing Everest in a Lycra stretch suit. Freeze-dried food was eaten the whole way, not so much as a book or a music tape for entertainment, no proper way to wash yourself —

all in the interest of saving weight. One guy in the last race had said if dogs lived like the round-the-world race sailors, the ASPCA would bust the owners. All participants would acknowledge that the Geneva Convention demanded a better lifestyle for prisoners. And Koonce had done this race not once, but three times. It required a certain kind of madness. It also required a high level of skill and seamanship, and an unfettered passion for the adventurous life that every sailor in the yacht club wished he had more of.

As if winning The Race, as it was called, wasn't enough, Koonce had come close to winning the America's Cup for New Zealand. The two events couldn't be any more different. The Race demanded great self-discipline, ultimate endurance, serious toughness. The America's Cup was match racing, day sailing around buoys. The logistics and politics ashore were just as tough as the hand-to-hand combat on the racecourse. Doing the America's Cup was like a Silicon Valley start-up. It called for leadership, diplomacy, media manipulation, and public relations as well as coordinating a design team on land and a sailing team of sixteen on the water. Sailing credentials didn't get much better than those carried by Alistair Koonce.

Andy watched him field questions from the sailors at the table, and found it difficult not to admire the guy. He had that terse, Kiwi way of keeping everything short, always looking for the touch of dry humor, downplaying his accomplishments, sticking to the facts. People who thought the Swedes were the ultimate stoics hadn't spent much time with the Kiwis. And Koonce was a classic example. But when you have the cards Koonce has, Andy thought, there's not much need for elaboration.

Mitchell hadn't said a word for a while. He had that "international host" look going, the plastic posture of tolerant generosity men like Mitchell Thomas affected when under the protective roof of their own exclusive clubs or executive offices. But Andy had the feeling Koonce was saving him for last. And it was getting to that point. The boys were all bug-eyed now from the Koonce show, all pumped up from having this rock star be so friendly, pay so much attention to them. He could turn on the charm, no question.

Deedee was just about vibrating off her chair under his gaze, which he was thoughtful enough to lavish in her direction, making points, finishing off thoughts, and mumbling asides as if they were just for her. Koonce was good, Andy thought, and he had done his homework.

"Here's a question for you," Koonce said to the sailors. They leaned forward, looking like a bunch of game-show contestants with their hands poised over their buttons. Andy got ready. Here it comes. "Where's America in all this?" The question was not delivered with hostility. The smile was still there, but the eyes were hard. Koonce paused, giving them too brief a moment to puzzle over the question. They were all too excited to react to this sudden, ominous shift in the breeze.

"Oh, I know America is involved," Koonce said, letting that last word linger on his tongue. "The race has stopped in Fort Lauderdale! And Baltimore. How about that! Oh yes, America loves the glamour of the boats coming in, the weary sailors home from the sea and all that. The hotel and restaurant revenues get a shot in the arm, the local politicos make hay at the parties, everybody loves the glitz of it, and of course the marketing tie-ins don't quit. But where are the American sailors? Where are the American-sponsored boats? The greatest ocean race in the world — one of the greatest sporting adventures in the world in any sport — and there are no American entries! Not one. Am I right? I am right about that, am I not?"

Professor Koonce waited until he had some half-hearted nods and grunts from the boys. As Koonce paused, Andy noticed that the noise level in the dining room had diminished considerably. Koonce's presence at the *Worthy* table had drawn glances. Now his little speech was focusing general attention. Koonce knew how to work a room. "It's hard to believe with all the great sailors in this country, and all the big money, and all the nautical pride and high-seas tradition that goes back to John Paul Jones and beyond, that there is not one man among you stout-hearted enough to mount a campaign to race around the world. What's happened to you Americans, you pioneers who took wagons across the Rocky Mountains, who hammered towns out of the desert, built impossible railroads and created the most powerful nation on earth? You have two hundred million people, and not one entry for The Race. Ever! It's astounding, appalling if you think about it."

Koonce laughed. He was on a roll. All eyes began drifting, inevitably, to Mitchell Thomas. But Koonce, ever the sportsman, gave his adversary a little breathing room. He had, after all, ambushed the man in his own club. If he didn't step back and let him up, he couldn't deck him again.

"I love racing like we did this week," Koonce said, his voice dropping into public-relations gratitude. "The competition was great, the weather was perfect, and at the end of each day we tidied up the yachts, whistled for the launch, and came in to this beautiful club for a drink or two, a hot shower, a delicious dinner, and a great night's sleep in clean sheets in the company of . . . loved ones." Koonce's smile was lecherous. He adjusted his necktie Rodney Dangerfield–style as a few people chuckled. "But The Race is something else again. It's man against the elements night and day for weeks at a time. Nowhere to hide. Teams of sailors whose pride is their resourcefulness, their courage, their perseverance to see it through, survive, race, win! It's basic stuff, true grit. It's a John Wayne movie, 'war without bullets,' as your famed skipper Ted Turner would say. He's never done The Race, has he? And the new sixty-footers, these are some ultimate boats, the Formula Ones of ocean racing. A great ride if your heart can take it. They've logged four hundred forty nine miles in twenty-four hours, a new monohull record under sail. That's a twenty-four-hour average of eighteen-point-seven knots. An average! Top speeds over thirty-two knots have been recorded. After that, people were too frantic to keep proper track. This is sailing on the edge, my friends. Nothing else comes close. How can you Americans not be there?"

Now the silence was deafening. No one in the dining room with its dark paneling, upon which hung oil paintings commemorating great moments in naval and yachting history, had missed the unmistakable drop of the gauntlet. And there was no mistaking, either, that it had landed smack in Mitchell Thomas's half-finished piece of apple pie à la mode. Koonce seemed frozen in time, his hands upheld to dispel any thought that this last question was rhetorical. Andy chose this moment to lean his head toward Isha and mutter something in her ear. Leaping gratefully at this diversion, Mitchell addressed his son in a cold voice as full of command and censure as he could manage.

"Do you have something to say we all might share, Andy?"

Quite drunk by now, Andy looked up, regarded Mitchell. His grin was sheepish. His words were only slightly slurred. "Sure, Mitchell. Sure. S'cuse me. Din' mean to be rude. I was jus' commenting to Isha here that this ocean race, The Race, sounds like your kind of project. Right up your alley." As he finished, Andy's head began nodding up and down like one of those bobblehead sports dolls people mounted on the dashboards of their automobiles. He might be nodding yet if someone hadn't begun clapping. At least five different people were later said to have started it. All denied being the culprit. But in seconds, the applause had built to a deafening level.

III

ELVES

The board room at Moss Optical was round with a high, deeply-domed ceiling. It was a small planetarium. The black walnut table that looked and felt like satin was fifteen feet across and shaped like a donut. There were twenty exotic-looking leather chairs around the table, thirty more around the perimeter of the room, all on rollers. Each one reclined nearly to a full horizontal position. Within the center space was a MossStar Heavens TR29 projector with the basic shape of a dumbbell. Round globes at each end that glittered with lenses were connected by an arm of structural steel that was attached to a base at its balance point. When not in use, the projector was hydraulically retracted into a work space beneath the floor. The projector was in a constant state of development. Moss engineers and scientists used it as a prototype for studying new ways to broadcast patterns of the universe that were accurate to the millisecond upon the midnight-blue ceiling. The MossStar Heavens TR29 was the best and most advanced instrument of its kind in the world.

The star shows at Moss Optical were legendary. The acoustics in the planetarium were perfect. The most quietly uttered aside could be heard anywhere in the room as if one's ear were next to the speaker's mouth. This unique, acoustical quality of the room had the effect of subduing all who entered. The audio track that accompanied the show was a tape loop made on one of the early space-shuttle voyages. It was the real, unaltered sound of outer space played back on the best stereo system available. With stars and planets projected on the ceiling, the narrator speaking in soothing, conversational tones, and the audio fingerprint of the universe providing the deepest, most riveting silence one could imagine, the effect was emotionally transporting. Anyone who had ever looked at the heavens with more than passing interest would covet an invitation to a Moss star show.

The planetarium was built by Deedee Moss's father. Randolph Moss was the founder, chief astronomer, chief engineer, and far and away the most avant-garde thinker in his company. Randolph Moss was a curious man, a touch daffy by all accounts, a night person whose fourteen-hour work days began in the late afternoon. A tall, angular man who never raised his voice, Moss never slept more than four hours a day, and that in twenty-minute cat naps. For a man who constantly challenged the technological barriers of his scientific field, he lived as a throwback to the previous century. He hated automobiles. He rode his bicycle the three miles to his office year round in all but the worst weather. On those days he allowed himself to be driven. He hated telephones too, but his pragmatism forced him to use them without restraint for business. People who worked with him learned to expect calls at all hours of the night. But for all his creative energy, Randolph Moss was prudish and narrow-minded in his personal life, a stickler for appearance, a man for whom formality was an essential crutch. His children were required to eat in the kitchen until they were old enough to dress properly and display polished manners at his table. An exuberant Dr. Jekyll in his laboratory by night, Randolph Moss was a stern, formidable husband and father at home.

Moss was well into his eighties when he figured out how to cast and polish the biggest lens that had ever been made for a telescope, a breakthrough that catapulted his company to the forefront of the optics industry. His accomplishment was no more astounding than his insistence that the solution had been brought to him by a group of elves as he worked alone in his lab one night. At least that was what he called what he described as opportune, cosmic messengers. Elves. And it wasn't a joke, although he did accept gentle teasing about it by a few close family members, and by ever fewer trusted friends and coworkers with whom he had shared this secret. He swore to the truth of it until the day he died at age ninety-six.

The board meetings of Moss Optical always concluded with a star show. It was a good way to bring members up to date on any new advances in Moss's most impressive (and most expensive) product, and frankly, it was one of the perks board members looked forward to the most, a close second only to stock options. As the business of the board concluded on this particular day, the distinguished men and women around the table relaxed visibly as one, chatting quietly as they returned their paperwork to leather cases, and caressed the "recline" buttons on their chairs with anticipation.

But when the slide in the floor in the center of the donut table opened, and the hushed whir of machinery was heard, it was not the MossStar Heavens TR29 that appeared. It was a multi-faceted, translucent ball eight feet in diameter that ascended on the thinnest possible pedestal. This was the MossScreen 2000, a digital system capable of projecting images, still or video, simultaneously on all four quadrants of the ball without the slightest distortion. So new was this fiber-optical prototype that the board members were only vaguely familiar with the concept that had been presented to them by Moss scientists several years before. While they were collectively marveling over this latest bit of futuristic fantasy, Sam Cotton cleared his throat and began to speak.

In the chair beside Sam Cotton, Deedee Moss came to life. As the founder's daughter and majority stockholder, Deedee was a member of the Moss board in perpetuity. To her credit, she rarely missed a meeting. But while she was there in body, her spirit often flagged under the drone of numbers and tiresome reports. She had no desire to participate in the management of Moss. Her husband, Mitchell, took care of that. She simply felt a family responsibility to carry the flag, keep the Moss name alive. That would please her father, she knew. After her, it would have to be Andy. She hoped he would be willing to carry the flag. He wasn't very interested in the company, she knew that. She hoped it would grow on him. He did love astronomy. He got that directly from his grandfather. She never failed to think about Andy replacing her as she sat in her father's beloved planetarium room, usually just before she dozed off, which was predictably within the first ten minutes of a meeting. Deedee dozed the way she did everything — with dignity. New members had a hard time discerning that she was napping. Her head was inclined gently back against the rest, eyes closed perhaps in contemplation, and her hands were relaxed on the arms of the marvelously comfortable, soft leather chair. Only her stillness and measured breathing betrayed her withdrawal from the proceedings.

As the meeting concluded and the MossScreen 2000 made its appearance, Deedee awoke, a transition she always managed without the slightest twitch or shudder. She simply opened her eyes. But as Sam Cotton began speaking, she was more than awake. She was involved. For the Deedee Moss–watchers among the board members, and there were several, the sudden interest on her part was a red flag.

Sam Cotton, the Moss family attorney for decades, was in his late seventies. He was less than six feet tall, formerly a bundle of muscle who had played rugby at Harvard. At seventy-four he had shot his age on the golf course, a lifelong dream. But lately Sam had been struggling with a succession of illnesses, and a revisitation of old injuries, that had softened the edge of his physique. Fatigue haunted his features. He'd finally quit his thrice-weekly tennis foursome. But other than a couple brief hospitalizations, Sam hadn't missed a day at the office. Sam figured it was okay to leave the game, but while you remained, you'd better keep playing your hardest. He was also a member of the Moss board, there mainly to look out for Deedee's interests. This day, Sam had arranged with the chairman to have a few minutes after the business meeting for a presentation.

The lights dimmed in the room as Sam Cotton began to speak.

"Mrs. Thomas has asked me to present a project she would very much like the company to undertake."

Board members came to full attention, because this was a first. Not even the most senior among them could recall input or even participation of any sort from Deedee Moss Thomas.

An image appeared on the MossScreen 2000. It was a low-altitude aerial photograph of a large, racy-looking sailboat in full cry. It was shot from the side, showing the bow of the boat overhanging a gigantic wave by at least twenty feet as it took off, trying to fly as it was struck by a fierce gust of wind. Sam paused, allowing the members to savor the extraordinary image. After a few seconds, the video came to life, showing the boat completing its drop off the wave and practically disappearing in the deluge of green and white water scooped up by the bow. Sam waited for the chorus of exclamations to recede. The video now was showing a model of the extraordinary boat from various angles.

"This is a World 60, a class that has evolved from twenty-five years of racing boats around the world. It's actually sixty-three feet overall. The mast tip is eighty-four feet above the deck. The boat weighs less than most forty-footers, with more than half that weight in the keel. It may look like a day boat, but a crew of twelve people race these things around the world—thirty thousand miles, starting and finishing in Southampton, England, leaving the continents to port. The Race, as it is called, takes nine months."

As Sam spoke, the board secretary circled the table passing out a packet of information. The video segued to a montage of shore activity.

"There are between six and eight stopovers each race in places like Australia, New Zealand, Brazil, Uruguay, the U.S., France, England, and Sweden to allow for re-provisioning, repairs, and crew rest and recreation, although I'm told there is precious little of the latter. A typical stopover is two weeks, and as you can see, that time is used to excellent advantage by sponsors of the various yachts. Social events, client activities like day sails on the boats, and a variety of other business-related gatherings are centered on this rather spectacular, romantic adventure.

"There's much more, but I suggest you read the information Sally has distributed, no need taking up your time here. The basic proposal is for us to sponsor one of these boats, making it the Moss flagship, and launching it on its way around the world. Then it's up to us to make the most of it through a well-planned campaign of advertising and promotion. To answer the most obvious questions, sponsorship of an entry costs around fifteen million and change. That covers design and construction of two boats, which I am told is essential to be competitive; crew salaries—the sailors are pros, and they'll be working two straight years on this project—spare parts, sails, a shore crew that travels to each port, food, clothing, the works.

"Does it pay off? There's no easy answer to that. We'd be allowed to use the boat as a floating billboard for Moss, with our logo plastered on sails, hull, deck, and uniforms. In addition to worldwide print coverage, the TV is excellent, including ESPN here at home. In your packets you will find some compelling studies various sponsors have released to show the miracles wrought by international publicity for their brand image. My own feeling is that it depends on the company. For us, it is an opportunity not only for brand exposure through the world, but to give our binocular and telescope lines a huge boost. I have been assured that if Moss were to sponsor a boat, our company would be named the official provider of optics for the fleet.

"One more thing. There has never been an American boat in this race. A couple hundred Americans have sailed on the race, but never on a U.S. boat. We have an opportunity to sponsor the first American entry ever in The Race around the world. That in itself would make Moss the focus of considerable attention."

The room was silent after Sam finished. Many of the board members flipped through the information packet as the lights came up and the MossScreen 2000 sank quietly out of sight. Deedee said nothing. She didn't need to. She was glowing.

One board member managed to find his voice. "So, will you skipper the boat?" From across the table, the question was directed at Mitchell Thomas, who was seated on the side opposite his wife.

Mitchell smiled, shook his head. "I wish I could. But I don't see how I could take the time off this project would require. And as Sam said, this is a game for professionals. But I assure you I will find the best possible man for the job . . . if the board approves, of course."

Mitchell's stamp of approval was unmistakable. There were no more questions. The lights dimmed, putting the planetarium in total darkness as the MossStar Heavens TR29 rose from beneath the floor. Deedee pressed the "recline" button on her chair. This was one of the favorite moments in her life, the main reason she never missed a meeting. She never tilted back in her chair without feeling twelve years old, her age when the planetarium first opened, when she was nearly overcome by the experience. Every show was like the first time for her. Every time she felt herself being swallowed up by the overwhelming silence of deep space, tears welled in her eyes and the top of her head prickled. And now The Race. Oh, how she hoped the board would approve.

IV

SHANGHAIED

The parking lot of Jan Sargent's Mondo Sports office on North Draper Avenue in San Diego was crowded with TV vans. As usual, every station in town had responded to Sargent's announcement of a press conference. It would take a major military flare-up somewhere in the world, or a particularly juicy political scandal at City Hall, to keep the TV crews away from a Sargent press conference. The two-time America's Cup winner was the most colorful sailor to come along since Ted Turner, whom Koonce had mentioned in his speech at the New York Yacht Club. Sargent could run the gamut of mean, nasty, vindictive, funny, and charming in a single sentence. The only sure thing about Sargent was that he never let a news crew down. Unlike so many professional sailors, who could be more politically correct than the original astronauts, Jan Sargent always fired from the hip. When Sargent was on a roll, even innocent bystanders had been known to catch a slug.

Nobody loved holding a press conference more than Jan Sargent. The sight of several thirty-pound, hundred-and-fifty-thousand-dollar professional Betacams leveled at him from their perches on sturdy tripods, their cold, unblinking eyes ready to bring his most subtle expressions, his every twist and turn of phrase into the living rooms of hundreds of thousands of homes, was second only to the one-minute signal on a crowded, wind-blown starting line for the adrenaline rush it produced. When the sound guy clipped that little lavalier mike to his shirt and ran the wire under his clothing, Jan Sargent always broke a light sweat. It was like being handed a fully loaded automatic weapon. When the presenter stepped up and delivered that first question, he was as psyched as any hitter who ever faced major-league pitching in a clutch situation.

Jan Sargent's office was a virtual sound stage, from the eye-catching arrangement of trophies, half-models, and photographs crowding the TV-friendly blue wall behind his desk to the color-balanced track lighting in the ceiling that had been installed by cinematic specialists from Los Angeles. The tail of the hidden, broadcast-quality microphone on his desk terminated in a panel that was accessible behind a hinged door on the front of the desk, and that accommodated sound plugs from eight cameras. There was a private side entrance to Sargent's office from the bathroom. When all was in readiness, Sargent could take a last approving look at the effect he was after, and make his entrance. Doris, his secretary, had taken a course in the cosmetic arts. Jan

Sargent had taken a course in public speaking, not that he really needed it. He was a natural.

He had called the press conference to announce his acquisition of a major sponsor for his America's Cup campaign that would come to fruition four years hence. It was a coup to have a major sponsor on board so early, and Sargent had played it to the hilt. He'd taken a few light shots at the other, less fortunate American syndicates—"pretenders" he'd called them—praised his sponsor's good judgment, and now he was fielding questions.

"Ed Tower, WETX. Are you planning a two-boat campaign?"

Sargent turned his large head a few degrees and leveled a glance at Tower. It was the eyes that had it. Sargent's eyes were stone cold no matter what emotions or theatrics the rest of his face was exhibiting. He could be laughing, frowning, being surprised, but the eyes never changed. The voice was that of a detective questioning a murder suspect.

"Ed, how many America's Cups have you covered?"

"Three. No. Four."

"Wouldn't you say that anything but a two-boat campaign would be stupid?"

As the assembled media chuckled, Sargent was distracted by Doris, who had slipped into the room via the side door. Sargent motioned her to his desk. She handed him a slip of paper and left.

"Okay guys, I have to take this phone call. Cameras off. But you can stay, no problem. You might find it interesting. I might find it interesting." Sargent picked up the telephone. Talking on the phone in front of an audience was one of his favorite gambits. He was a master at it.

"Mitchell Thomas! How's my favorite Corinthian! Did I receive the shipment of binoculars you sent for my America's Cup crew? No, not yet. But how thoughtful of you."

Sargent exchanged a wink with Ed Tower, reeling him back in after making him look foolish. That was Jan Sargent's game. He went one-on-one with everyone. It was how he kept control. He had a personal relationship with each of the reporters in the room just as he did with each man on his crew, and with each person in his company. He dealt with everyone privately. That way no one knew what he had to say to anyone else. Each person knew where he stood with Sargent, but not in relation to where anyone else stood. Divide and conquer. Only Sargent had the full picture. Only Sargent had the reins.

"What am I doing? I'm in the middle of a press conference. I just announced the Gaflack Communications sponsorship. Five million. Not too shabby, eh? That's more than you're writing me a check for, Mitchell. About five million more." Sargent mimed a big silent laugh for his attentive audience.

"So how'd you do in Newport?" He aimed cagey smile at the troops, indicating that he knew very well down to the last detail how Mitchell Thomas had done in Newport, down to the last crossing tack of the last race when Alistair Koonce had nearly cut him in half.

"Yeah, I heard you nearly got him in that last race. Must have been close. A little too close maybe . . . " Sargent rolled his eyes.

"Okay, I'm listening."

For several minutes Sargent listened, long enough

for the news crews to tire of the game and begin looking at their watches. Sargent took no notes. He didn't believe in notes. Notes could only come back to haunt you. His brain was the only recorder he needed.

"Interesting. Very interesting . . . no, it's not out of the question at all . . . give me a day to think about it . . . no, I understand . . . I'll give you my thoughts tomorrow . . . good . . . okay, Mitchell . . . "

Sargent hung up, serious now as he turned to face the cameras.

"You might want to roll on this." He paused as camera crews came to attention, did sound checks, got their equipment rolling.

"All set?"

"I would like you all to be the first to know that I have just been invited to skipper a boat in the ocean race around the world. The Race. My invitation comes from Mitchell Thomas, who announced last week that his company, Moss Optics, planned to sponsor the first American boat ever to enter this race."

Sargent paused.

"Any questions?"

Eight reporters started talking at once.

"Man, you should see Andrea today. Hair all piled up on her head. And a dress we've never seen. Red. Slinky. Pretty rad for the office. My God that woman is built. Come look."

"Can't." Andy was slumped at his desk on the twenty-fourth floor of Moss Optic's Manhattan headquarters, head in hands. His office was a shambles of stacked boxes. It looked as if no one had done a thing since the movers had left three weeks ago, but it did show signs of habitation. Old soft-drink cups languished on windowsills and tables among piles of magazines and newspapers. Andy's desk was buried. It wasn't the clutter of nonstop business. It was the dusty disarray of neglect.

Jeff Linn, Andy's best friend in the company, was staring intently into the eyepiece of a small, deceptively powerful telescope mounted on a tripod near the window. An opticist, Jeff had been the creative force behind the development of the Moss Stealth Scope that he was now using to peer into offices and apartments scores of blocks away. What better use for such a marvelous instrument, Jeff had once asked Andy. Andy couldn't think of one. The two were high-tech peeping Toms, giving their favorite subjects names, fantasizing about their jobs, lives, and relationships. "Andrea" was a favorite of Andy's. But Andy looked broken. Even the promise of Andrea's new look couldn't distract him.

"I need a drink."

"This is better than booze. She just stood up. She's fixing her scarf . . . "

"Shut up, man. I'm dying here. I've been shanghaied, knocked senseless, dumped in a sack, and heaved on board this goddamn boat, trapped like a rat, hemmed in on all sides. It's like being put on board the Titanic when you know before you board that it's going to go down. Maybe my boat isn't going down, but it may as well. I'd rather the thing went down right after the start so I wouldn't be tortured for nine months. Nine months is a long time to be tortured."

Andy got up and began pacing. "How the hell did this happen to me, Jeff? Hey, it's me, Andy Thomas, gentleman alcoholic, playboy in training, poor little rich guy doin' the best he can, hiding away in the heavens with his books, his dogs, his high-maintenance trophy girlfriend who treats him like a hostage, and Momma Deedee who regularly saves his ass and makes it all possible. What's gone wrong? Where's Momma Deedee when I need her? Something is strange here, man. She's avoiding me. She says talk with Mitchell. Talk with Mitchell? There's a first. Why is she so fixated on this goddamn race? Without her running interference Mitchell is gonna ride me right into the ground. He's got a rope around my nuts and he's lovin' it."

Jeff took his eye away from the scope and regarded his friend. Andy walked over, bent to the eyepiece.

"My luck, she's gone . . . no, here she comes, wow, you're right, lookin' good, mighty good. What a class act of a babe. What a piece of work, this scope. Look at that image. It feels as if I could speak to her. How far away are we? A mile? You're a freaking genius, Jeffie."

"Thanks. But it never would have worked without your input. I'd say it's about a mile."

Andy straightened up, looked at Jeff, and resumed his pacing. "If you're such a genius, help get me out of this mess. Can you see me doing this? Come on . . . me, taking off into the briny trapped in a thirty-five-foot plastic tube with eleven gung-ho animals for nine months, so bad out there most days that you can't even brush your teeth let alone wash your pits, tryin' to take a dump over the side while the boat's being whipped around like a rag in the mouth of a crazed terrier . . . "

"I thoughts the boats were sixty-five feet."

Andy stopped pacing. "They are, but you got to keep weight out of both ends. Weight in the ends slows a boat down, makes it pitch. So everybody lives and works in the middle of the boat."

"I see."

Andy laughed at how easily Jeff could sidetrack him. Bloody scientists. He began pacing again. "I'm glad you see it, Jeffie, because it's all a goddamn blur to me. How about the Southern Ocean, Drake Passage, Cape Horn? Sounds cool, doesn't it? Magic names. The stuff of romance for landlubbers like you. Well, I've seen the videos on ESPN, talked to a couple of the poor slobs who have done this race. There's nothing romantic about it when you're the guy in charge of providing romantic visions for future generations. You're freezin' ass out there, colder than you ever thought you could be, and for weeks at a time. There's no place to hide. The deck in twenty-five to fifty knots of wind and huge seas looks like a combat zone. The water flying off the bow knocks guys right off their feet. Below decks is like a swamp in winter. You're out of the wind, and it's a little warmer if the heater isn't broken, which I'm told it usually is, but not enough to get the chill out of your bones. And that's when everything is running smoothly. Now the odd wave smacks your stern at the same time you catch a gust of wind in the forty-knot range, and all hell breaks loose. You spin out, with the boat pinned on its side by a spinnaker full of wind, then water; mast parallel with the horizon. You know what you do then, Jeffie? You hang by your thumbs and wait for the spinnaker to rip apart. No, you pray for it to rip apart. That can take several minutes, a lifetime when you are laid over ninety-degrees. When the chute finally rips apart, the water dumps out and the boat rights itself. Then you hurry to clean up the mess, working with twenty pounds of wet clothes on, boots full of water, hands numb, because you've got to get another spinnaker up. Why? Because you're racing! This isn't a leisurely cruise around the world. It's brutal, man. The ESPN shows us onboard footage. I've seen it!"

Andy paused, but kept pacing, getting more worked up.

"An average of two boats per race lose masts. Crunch, smacko, down they came. Two thousand miles from nowhere, with no mast. People probably hurt. People like me, Jeffie."

Jeff buried his head in the telescope. There was nothing he could think of to say.

"What do they eat? Nothing but freeze-dried food. Ever eat any of that junk? It's like glue. We're talking impaction. Ruins your health for years afterwards. Why? To save weight. Madness.

"And ice! Oh yeah, let's not forget about the ice. You're screaming along at twenty-five knots boat speed at night in the middle of the Southern Ocean. Ever look at the map? That ocean circles the globe at around forty degrees south, unimpeded . . . no land in the way to slow down the weather. I've seen videos of crews sailing the Southern Ocean in a damn blizzard — can't see to the front of the boat the snow is coming so thick. You've got a face mask and goggles on, and it's lucky that everything including your brain is half-frozen because if you could think, here's what you'd be thinking about: growlers. You know what a growler is, Jeffie? It's a chunk of ice that breaks off a big berg. A chunk the size of a pickup truck. Solid as concrete. It floats just above or below the surface. Think about hitting one of those at twenty-five knots . . . or a freaking container! Hundreds of those things fall off ships every year."

Andy slumped into his chair, the picture of dejection. His sudden laugh sounded hollow. "It's like riding a motorcycle through a minefield at high speed. That's what these guys do . . . me! . . . that's what I'm going to be doing unless we can think of something. Come on, man. Help me out here."

"You could always shoot yourself in the foot," Jeff said quietly, not taking his eye off the scope. "My older brother says a friend of his did that in the sixties to keep from going to Nam."

Andy let his head fall to the desk. His eyes were closed. He imagined pointing a gun at his foot, the old bolt-action .22 caliber rifle he used for shooting squirrels off the bird feeder. The muzzle of the long barrel would be inches from his foot. The right one? No, the left. Would he take his shoe and sock off, watch the hole appear in his foot as he fired, watch the foot jerk as the bullet hit it, watch the blood splatter . . . ? No, leave the sock on, like the hood they put over the head of somebody about to be executed. Give the poor foot that much dignity. But no need ruining the shoe. Although with a bullet hole, it would make a nice trophy. Bam! He heard the distant echo of another shot, one fired in a tunnel a long time ago. A wave of nausea crawled past. Shoot himself in the foot? Who was he kidding. With his luck it would get infected and they'd have to cut it off. No way. The intercom buzzed. Andy ignored it. It buzzed again.

Andy didn't move. He wondered if he might be unconscious. A third buzz. Bad sound. He managed to move one hand and find the intercom button. "Yes, Gloria." His mouth was mashed into several layers of newspaper on his desk. His voice sounded muffled, foreign to him.

"Your father would like to see you, Andy."

V

ULTIMATUM

Andy treasured Gloria. She let him know what it would be like to have a sister; an older, very mean sister. Having Gloria close by reaffirmed his eternal gratitude for only-childhood. Gloria was such a company girl. And a knockout, as bad luck would have it. If ever a woman should have been born ugly, it was Gloria. Her glossy plumage gave her terrible power. She was maddeningly efficient, totally capable. She had the energy of a squirrel in heat. She did Andy's work, and more pool work than any other girl in the office. She had all the humor of a blackberry hedge. She ran five miles every day and was famous for beating the crap out of most of the men she was able to lure onto the tennis court. She had no trouble finding opponents. Gloria in a tennis dress was maga-zine quality. And her formula worked. The tougher the opponent, the more revealing the dress. She was a spider woman, black widow variety. Toward the end of a match going in her favor she would outwardly gloat. "Too bad," she would say when an opponent's shot missed the mark. "Oh, too bad." Talk about killer instinct. The cat with the mouse. The thought of having sex with Gloria was both stimulating and frightening. If anyone Andy knew had ever scored with her, it had been too painful for them to admit it.

"Now, Andy."

"Yes, Gloria."

Andy got up, snugged his necktie into place, put on a jacket, ran a hand through his hair. No need being out of uniform. Not that it mattered. He had no cards. Not a one.

"I have no cards," he said to Jeff.

"I'll try to think of something. I will. Sorry about the foot idea."

"Hey, it's not bad. This is an emergency. And I can't come up with anything better. So . . . " Andy pointed an imaginary rifle at his left foot, aimed with care, and said "Bang." He grimaced in pain, dramatically feigned handing a gun to Jeff, who, like a good buddy, reached out and took it. Then Andy hopped out the door on one foot, murmuring, "Ow . . . ow . . . ow." As he passed Gloria's desk, her eyes never left her computer screen.

"Hurt yourself?"

"Yes, I shot myself in the foot."

"Not the first time."

"And," Andy said with a radiant smile, "certainly not the last." Gloria looked up, caught the smile as she rushed the net, and put it away with a crisp smile of her own.

Andy hopped all the way to his father's office, a distance of twenty-five yards that were thickly carpeted in deep-blue pile with patterns of various constellations interwoven in silver thread. He hopped past the copier room, over the big dipper, past the offices of two vice presidents with their tightly coiffed guard-dog secretaries stationed outside, over Uranus, past the huge black-and-white photographs of Moss products, past a glass-walled conference room where a large portrait of his grandfather was strategically hung for maximum impact, and finally to his father's command compound, where Superwoman and her sister flanked the entrance to Mitchell's inner sanctum. A pair of elite Mossad guards with Uzis hanging from their shoulders wouldn't have been more intimidating than these women. Andy had always wondered where Moss secretaries came from, especially his father's. If one left for some reason, another from the same mold would appear as if by magic. They were always tall, in their forties, very sanitary. Their clothes were tailored to uniform proportions. They reminded him of the statuesque, imposing women from the movie *She*, something he'd seen on TV at two a.m. one sleepless night — "She who must be obeyed." Ursula Andress had played the title role. But those Amazonian babes were sex on the hoof. Both of his father's secretaries were robotic, projecting that same icy charm professional killers had before they calmly shot you between the eyes, nothing personal, pal. He was sure they were cloned in a secret facility buried beneath the fields of a secluded farm in the wastelands of North Dakota. If the aliens ever took over, it would start right here at Moss. How appropriate. It was an X-file waiting to be opened.

Andy hopped to a halt equidistant from the two women. They looked up as one, and as one they chose to ignore his one-legged arrival, an exertion that was now causing him to breathe heavily and break a sweat. He looked expectantly from one to the other like a man overboard in need of a life ring.

"Hello, Andy," said the one on his left. Was there rank involved, or was it her turn? He never knew. "Your father is waiting. Please go right in. Can I bring you coffee, tea?"

"How about a hunk of raw meat," Andy said, and hopped in to Mitchell's den.

Andy didn't see much of Mitchell at the office, mainly because Andy didn't spend a lot of time there. His mother insisted he work for the company, hoping against hope that he would get attached to the place by osmosis. She thought it was just as important to have a Moss on the executive staff as it was to have one on the board, and she and Andy were all that was left of the line. Mitchell hated the idea. He didn't want Andy anywhere near the place. All he could manage to do was convince Deedee that to uphold company morale, Andy had to put in his time. If he didn't, his paychecks would be withheld. That was a joke. Andy had plenty of his own money, and Deedee always slipped him extra from her personal account.

Andy was smart. When he'd finally started paying attention his last two years in college, he'd aced astronomy, making the dean's list and winning an academic award in the process. People said he had a slice of his grandfather's creative bent. People who had known the old man said that in many ways Andy was just as eccentric. That was the most polite word they used. Whether the office was a true enigma to him, as it had been to his grandfather, or whether Andy was just using that as a ruse to absent himself from the bother of work, no one quite knew. Or maybe it was just Mitchell.

Mitchell was looking out the window with his back to the elegant saloon that was his office. When he heard the thump, thump of Andy's arrival, he turned.

"Something wrong?"

"I shot myself in the foot."

A curious smile spread across Mitchell's face. Then he laughed, a short, staccato burst.

"You don't have the guts."

"You're right about that." Andy's foot was suddenly cured. He placed it gingerly on the rug, put some weight on it. It felt fine. He shrugged.

He watched as Mitchell slipped behind his French campaign desk that was supposed to have been lugged around by Napoleon's lackeys, talk about the right piece of furniture for this guy, and settled himself in his ornate captain's chair that had come off of the great schooner Atlantic, transatlantic record holder from 1905 to 1980. He shot his cuffs so his gold, Tony Correa monkey's paw links were displayed properly beyond the sleeves of his Armani double-breasted navy blazer, put his elbows on the table and clasped his hands. It was his patented getting-ready move. Andy was always surprised when Mitchell began with something other than, "My fellow Americans . . . "

Mitchell began talking about the race. He went on about Jan Sargent, who had agreed to skipper the boat, and the two-boat program that designer Gibb Frey was directing, and crew selection, on and on. The whole issue was so abhorrent to him that Andy had trouble focusing. Mitchell might have been babbling in Latin. That this nightmare fantasy was on the verge of becoming reality was too big a leap for him. His body suspended disbelief by refusing to sit still. Mitchell went down a long list, dwelling on small details with great enthusiasm, seeming to delight in Andy's discomfort. Pummeling him in his best booming voice with words, numbers, facts, names, and decisions, tightening the snare ever so slowly and with obvious relish. All that was missing, Andy thought, was a high-intensity light pointed at his face.

Try as he might, Andy could not escape this verbal barrage. He scanned the familiar room, looking for objects that might distract him, but found nothing. The big antique globe in the corner was now emblazoned with a red circumnavigation line of the racecourse. From where he sat, the red line came within an inch of Antarctica. On an easel where Mitchell usually kept some dreary painting he was considering buying, there was a flip-stack of designs for the boat. Sample crew clothing and foul-weather gear with Moss logos and the company slogan, "Do you really see?" embroidered under the boat's name, *All American*, were draped over chairs. The Race posters were spread out on Mitchell's big table.

Finally the man shut up for a moment. The sudden silence got Andy's attention. From Mitchell's look, he was waiting for a response. He must have ended with a question. He had to say something.

"I don't know, but it sounds great, Mitchell. Really

great. Listen, I have an idea. Since you're so into it, why don't you go? I'm just an also-ran, a nobody. I'm not cut out for this stuff. But you, you're a cool sailor, the hottest amateur around, a Corinthian's Corinthian, everyone knows that. Think of what a feather in your cap this would be . . . amateur skipper of the first American around-the-world boat. Mitchell Thomas! Ta-da! The cover of all the yachting magazines. Big profile in *The New York Times*. Interviewed on ESPN by Gary Jobson. On *Nightline* with Ted Koppel. You'd be a one-man media blitz. You'd be famous even if you came in last, perish the thought. And what if you won! Think of it. You'd have the first ticker-tape parade on Wall Street since the Stephens brothers won the transatlantic race in 1931. Baba Wawa would come calling. Letterman. Larry King. You'd be the toast of the yachting world, your name would be on everyone's lips, Moss binoculars on every coffee table. What a coup . . . "

Andy closely watched Mitchell's face as he laid it on and saw nothing. Not a flicker.

"Kind of you to paint such a glorious picture for me, Andy, and I have to admit that I am sorely tempted by the chance to co-skipper with the likes of Sargent. But unlike you, my boy, I have work to do, this company to run." Mitchell rubbed his hands together like a mechanic using a de-greasing cream. Andy often thought his father was the only person he'd ever met who could strut sitting down. "How will you be able to continue living in the manner to which you are accustomed if I let this old ship sink beneath the waves? I know having you away for so long will be a trial for all of us here because you are such an important player. Yes indeed, your absence will make it difficult, but we'll all pull extra hard and we'll make it through."

Andy let his head slump. He felt like a man who'd just been told he had six months to live. No possible cure. This was a done deal. He was right. He had no cards. His left foot twitched. This was so wrong, so misguided, like being incarcerated for something you couldn't possible have done, a classic case of mistaken identity. His mind was overcome with the heavy metal sound of barred doors closing, dozens of them, one behind the other. Begging was all that was left. This man, his father, had to have a heart in there somewhere. In twenty-five years he'd never encountered it, but hell, the man had a goddamn pulse, he'd seen his blood. He definitely wasn't some kind of alien pretender.

"Mitchell," he began in his most desperate voice, lifting his head and meeting Mitchell's eyes with considerable effort, "this is not me. I am a square peg in a round hole when it comes to racing around the world. I'm totally serious. Asking me to go on this race is like asking you to wear a dress to the next regatta party. It's not a fit. I will be a detriment to the crew. I am an ant at this picnic. You must reconsider. I don't know why you are so insistent that I go on the boat. Let me work on logistics, or sails, or run the shore team, whatever, but please, don't put me on the boat."

Mitchell let Andy finish. He was sitting back in his chair, relaxed, looking at Andy with ill-concealed distaste. Andy had seen people looking at dog vomit on their living room rug with more warmth. Inside, Andy shivered. This chunk of ice was his father. Mitchell the growler. And he was right in his path. Unavoidable. It was difficult to fathom. With a father like this, who needed enemies?

Mitchell leaned forward slowly, put one elbow on the desk, jutted his head toward Andy like an animal about to attack. His voice was low, measured.

"Now listen to me, because I am only going to say this once. You have never in your life finished anything you started. You have never had the balls to tackle anything tougher than a glass of expensive Scotch. You have gone through your pitiful existence taking the easy way out time after time. You were born rich. You're a mommy's boy, and your sweet little mommy has bailed you out of every uncomfortable situation you have ever gotten yourself into. And there have been many. I have tried to stop her from doing this, and failed. But not . . . this . . . time."

Mitchell's smile was thin and vengeful. It smacked of long-awaited victory.

"You are going on The Race. You will do every god-damn mile of this race, and you will either sink or swim, you will either be broken or survive. And afterward you will thank me. I hold you responsible for getting me — and Moss Optics — into this mess. It will cost this company fifteen million dollars because of your loose, drunken mouth at that dinner two months ago when Alistair Koonce put on his little show. So you will go on the race and carry the flag that was put up because you couldn't shut up. And maybe if you are out there mid-ocean, and another boat is on a collision course with you, you will think twice about telling the skipper there is no fucking problem when in fact the other guy is in a position to cut you in half. Maybe you will learn a lot of things out there.

"And if you should decide to bail out by shooting yourself in the foot or some other cowardly scam, I swear to you that I will pull the Moss sponsorship and scuttle the boat and I will let the whole world know that it was your doing. If that doesn't have sufficient impact you should know this: your dear mother is as insistent about you going as I am. No, actually, I would say that she is more insistent. And I know you wouldn't dream of disappointing her. So there you have it. Case closed."

Mitchell sat back, observing Andy like a research assistant regards a rat he has just injected with a deadly virus. Andy's head was swimming. He felt very bad.

"I . . . need some time . . . "

"Fine," Mitchell Thomas said expansively. "You have until Monday, when crew training begins at the Outward Bound School in Maine."

VI

ESCAPE

Andy was momentarily distracted by the familiar sight of the huge, freestanding oak tree on the big lawn seeming to rotate slowly on its base like a carousel as he passed by in the golf cart. It was one of his first and most magical memories of the sumptuous Long Island family estate where he had spent his youth. Most of his memories of those days were confusing, strangely disturbing, best left dormant. But he had gravitated to the shady strength of the oak not long after he learned to walk. Whenever he was missing, his parents knew where to find him. The tree was bigger now, but not all that much bigger. It was well over a hundred years old when he was born, a huge towering tree with an enormously thick trunk.

The golf cart lurched as it went off the concrete path. Andy reached out and steadied the wheel. His mother was driving. She wouldn't dream of driving a car, but she loved driving golf carts and boats. She gently pushed his hand away. "Everything's under control," she said, feigning admonishment with a little smile. Andy smiled back, knowing better. He couldn't understand what had happened to his mother. In his teens he had discovered the old scrapbooks hidden away in her bedroom, seen the pictures of her as a young girl, sailing, playing tennis. She looked so fit, so athletic. But he'd never known her as anything but sickly, tired, old-looking beyond her years. Now she was damn near a hermit, slogging through life in a dreary sort of way. She had no friends that he knew about, no interests other than the charities she supported.

He wondered what she did every day, what she thought about. But that regal way of hers made her impenetrable. She had locked all the doors and thrown away the keys long ago. And she always seemed so close to the edge of some kind of peril that one wouldn't dream of provoking even the mildest form of confrontation. The wave of sadness that struck Andy was so strong it caused him to forget just for a moment the reason he had come.

They were dressed all in white, mother and son. That was how she always went sailing, forever faithful to the family guidelines for how things were done. It was a wonder she didn't insist on high-button shoes, Andy thought. Surely they could be fitted with non-skid soles, for a price, and the price never mattered if it had to do with propriety. He'd never met people quite like his family. He was tutored at home when he first hit school age. After a few years even his grandfather had to relent, let the boy go off to a private day school where Andy had his first chance to compare notes with other kids and discover that his home environment was mighty strange.

It wasn't just the money. There were plenty of rich kids at the school. It was some heady extreme of self-proclaimed grandeur that his family had assumed. It was a sense of superiority, for sure, but it was more than that. There was a righteous isolation of body and spirit involved that was apparently designed to stop time, to preserve a certain moment of family prowess. What it really did was stunt growth and deny progress. Andy often wondered where the attitude originated, how it generated the power to sustain itself over so many years.

Perhaps aliens were involved, like those elves from outer space who supposedly helped his grandfather figure out how to cast that big telescope lens. His grandfather's combination of eccentricity and talent was a heavy card. And the wealth, of course. Anyone with that kind of power could call whatever tune he wanted, and when they did, everybody had better get up and dance. Powerful stuff. But it was his grandfather's chops that made people take him seriously. One couldn't quarrel with the accomplishments of Randolph Moss. Unfortunately, the rest of the family didn't inherit the chops, only the attitude, and the money to help sustain it. The missing piece was all too evident and it made the survivors seem quite ridiculous. Andy shot a glance at his mother, whose hands gripped the wheel and whose eyes were on the road, that little I'm-fine-thank-you smile firmly in place. She was going sailing.

The cart path led across the big lawn, through the exquisitely manicured gardens that were in full flower, past the tennis court, around the swimming pool with its quarter-scale version of the great house at one end, past the stables and indoor riding ring. What most people wouldn't give for this whole scene, Andy thought, and how classic it was that none of it interested him. He might have been a tourist trapped on a museum tour he hadn't signed up for.

When the path turned onto the paved road that led down the hill to the boathouse and dock, he got interested. The waterfront was a different story.

The twenty-six-foot custom day-sailor was at the dock. Andy had always loved the little boat, a gem that the legendary Nathanael Herreshoff had designed for his grandfather, a friend and fellow genius. Randolph Moss had named the boat *Katie*, after his wife. When the golf cart pulled into view, *Katie*'s mains'l began to go up as if by magic. Stoic old Karl Oyslebow, "Ossie" they called him, who had been in charge of the boathouse nearly fifty years, was on the job.

Ossie was Andy's first hero. His mother had taught him to sail, but Ossie, who had cut his teeth on fishing boats in his native Norway, had provided the grit of boats and water: the knot tying, the marlinspike seamanship, the secrets of paint and varnish, even some construction and repair techniques. And some basic understanding of marine engines. The stone boathouse that Ossie had built was the size of a good-sized barn, with a marine railway running into the big double doors on the water side. All the small boats were hauled out in the fall. Ossie spent winters getting them ready for the next season.

Oyslebow, who had come to the United States when his father had crewed on the America's Cup yachts of the 1930s, knew his stuff. And unlike Andy's father, he had time, patience, and some affection for the youngster. When he was moved to explore beyond the shade of the big oak, Andy headed for the waterfront and spent every available minute at the boathouse, watching and learning. But Andy had quit Oyslebow and the boat scene when he entered his teens, when the war with his father escalated, and when the game of escaping his old man's grasp became an obsession. He hadn't laid eyes on Ossie in a couple years. But then he only visited the estate when he absolutely had to. War was hell, and to make matters worse he was suddenly losing.

As unsteady as she was most of the time, Deedee stepped confidently onto the foredeck of the boat, took Ossie's hand, and stepped almost nimbly down into the cockpit, taking a seat in the stern next to the tiller. Andy's mother was never more at home than on a boat.

Oyslebow was more stooped than Andy remembered. He had to be into his mid-eighties now. But his shoulders were still powerful, his face no more craggy than always, his thick head of hair pure white. He was dressed the way he had always dressed, in the khaki uniform of the old-time paid hand. He wore the familiar leather knife kit on his hip, a knife sharp enough to keep his hair under control. The Moss house flag crossed with the burgee of the New York Yacht Club was embroidered on the front of his weathered cap. When Deedee thanked him for having the boat ready, he touched the visor of his hat but said nothing.

Andy waited on the dock. When Ossie stepped onto the foredeck, Andy put his foot on the bowline and gently applied pressure, slowly closing the distance between boat and dock. Then he stuck out his hand. Ossie looked at Andy in a way that made him feel naked before his old hero, embarrassed. Ossie looked at Andy's outstretched hand, cracked a grim smile, and reached for it. Andy felt the big crusty hand close on his like a vise as Ossie pulled himself onto the dock. Then he looked at Andy again at closer range. "How are ya?" he asked quietly, the pale-blue eyes calm. The question made a lump rise with surprising speed in Andy's throat. From the first time he entered the boathouse as a young boy, Ossie had been greeting him thus. And as always, Ossie already knew the answer. The old man turned away before Andy could gather his wits, walking off toward the boathouse and the familiar routine that awaited him.

Andy watched him go. He'd give anything to get inside Ossie's head. He'd tried a few times, but it was like pounding rocks. When it was about boats and the water, Ossie had always been an open book to him. But when it was about the family, he was a proverbial clam. Andy's grandfather had hired Oyslebow, pulled him out of a nasty situation, something about a fight one night in Newport, Rhode Island, when America's Cup Avenue was called Thames Street and lined with scummy bars full of tired hookers who would cut your heart out over ten bucks. Oyslebow was working for the famous Herreshoff boatyard at the time in Bristol, Rhode Island. There'd been some bad blood between Oyslebow and another worker that boiled over when the two met in a Thames Street bar. Oyslebow had put the other guy in the hospital. Nate Herreshoff, who had known Oyslebow, had passed on by then, but someone from the yard called Randolph Moss and asked him if he needed a good man to take care of his boats. It was either that or jail, or even extradition, for Oyslebow, who was a first-class craftsman. The old man was full of information that he would take to the grave out of loyalty to Randolph Moss.

"Coming?" Andy's mother was eager to cast off.

Like everything on the estate, *Katie* was immaculate, painted and varnished to a perfection that belied the boat's years. The lines were new, the sails sparkling white, the brass fittings gleaming. It was a sensual pleasure just being on *Katie* and using the gear. His mother busied herself organizing the lines while Andy raised the jib. They said nothing. The tasks had long ago been apportioned. Andy cast off and gave *Katie* a firm shove astern. Deedee put the tiller hard over to port as Andy backed the club-footed jib to starboard. As the boat turned away from the wind, Andy trimmed the sails and they accelerated out of the small, private harbor into Long Island Sound.

It was a gorgeous afternoon. The wind was blowing ten to twelve knots, just enough to raise a few little whitecaps, ideal conditions for the Herreshoff to sail fast without a fuss. The boat was well-balanced, so there was little pressure on the tiller. Deedee was beaming as she sailed *Katie* upwind, steering with two fingers, letting the boat have its head with only subtle corrections. Andy felt how lively the boat was, and admired his mother's touch on the helm. If she steered *Worthy* they'd never lose. That was a laugh. He could imagine how his father would accept that turn of events. Hey Mitch, by the way, today Mom will be on the helm upwind. Nothing personal, Dad, she's just a whole lot better than you. Oh yeah, what a scream that would be.

"We should tack." Andy had almost dozed off. They'd been sailing for almost an hour in silence before Deedee spoke quietly without taking her eyes off the jib telltales. She was sitting to leeward where she had a clear view of the jib under the mains'l, but mainly she loved the water skidding by so close to her shoulder. They were mid-sound. "Ready?" Deedee put the helm over gently, using all of the boat's momentum to swing through the wind in a smooth arc, losing a minimal amount of headway. As the boat settled onto the new tack, she expertly bore off the wind a few degrees, letting the boat get up to speed before she put it back in the upwind groove. Andy loved it. What a pleasure it was to watch someone so in tune with a fine sailboat.

"There are sandwiches in the cooler. And I should probably have a swig of my green medicine if you wouldn't mind."

Andy opened the cooler and brought out the bottle.

"Do you have a cup or something?"

"No, it's too bothersome. I just drink it from the bottle when no one is looking. Isn't that awful? And you don't count." She looked at Andy and smiled. He opened the bottle and handed it to her. No way was she going to relinquish the tiller even for the time it took to take her medicine. She took a gulp and handed it back.

"Horrible stuff." Deedee made a face as she licked her lips.

Andy returned the bottle to the cooler and took out a beer. It was time. He'd been lulled into simply enjoying this afternoon with his mother. But he had a mission.

"I've got to talk with you about this crazy race Mitchell has me going on," he said. "I was hoping I could explain my perspective of this thing and get you to help me make Mitchell understand how wrong it is for me. It's a bad idea, me going on this race."

"I'm really glad you brought it up, Andy."

"Really?" Andy's heart leapt. She was with him after all. Mitchell had been bullshitting as usual.

"Yes, because I know you are going to love it. You have to love it. I know you will."

Andy's heart landed with a thump in mid-leap. He was done for. This was his final appeal, and he could tell it was useless. He saw it in her face, heard it in her voice. She was the least aggressive, least demanding person he knew. But those few times when she had made up her mind it was set in concrete. He could talk to his mother until hell froze over and it wouldn't make a difference.

There had been other times he had failed to get his way with her. Not many. The jet ski was one. She even got furious when she saw him on a friend's. Hated the things. Saw them as unsuitable for anyone, let alone a member of the Moss family. Almost raised her voice about it. He could get himself in all kinds of trouble and she'd bail him out. She'd buy him anything, spoil him rotten. And always she'd step between him and Mitchell, take up for him even when his behavior was admittedly obnoxious. And never a big lecture. Just a mild correction when they were alone, and total support. But no disgusting jet ski. Didn't want to talk about it. Case closed.

Sailing lessons were the same. No excuse was good enough for missing a sailing lesson. The day he'd put a rusty nail through his foot she was waiting for him at the dock when he returned from the doctor. Sailing doesn't involve walking, she'd said. Anything less than perfection on the boat was unacceptable. The only good dock landing was one that touched the imaginary egg placed between dock and boat without breaking it. Sails had to be furled without a lump or a wrinkle. Sail trim had to be exact at all times. It was damn lucky he took to sailing. And now this.

"Mom . . ." He couldn't find the words. Why bother. He leaned against the coaming and took deep breaths, tried to beat back the panic that was creeping up like water in a flooding cellar. He tried to imagine anything worse than sailing around the world for nine months. Fury and despair wrestled to a standoff in his psyche. A wave of violence cruised through until his hand cramped from trying to crush the beer bottle like it were a can. Prison. That would be worse. That he managed to think of something worse brought relief. Not that nine months on a sixty-footer wasn't akin to imprisonment. At least he wouldn't get raped on The Race — as far as he knew.

Andy turned and observed his mother in total communication with the boat. "I know there's no point in discussing this, I know that. But there is one thing I'd like to know."

"What's that, Andy?"

"Why are you so sure I'm going to love it? You must have some reason for thinking that."

She looked at him for just a moment, and Andy saw a cloud flicker across her face like a sudden loss of power. Something strong, something ghostly had paid a visit. Her eyes returned quickly to the jib. For a moment she was silent.

"It's just a hunch, Andy. Just a hunch."

When she looked back at him, he thought her eyes were glistening a little too much.

"You have to remember, I know you better than you know yourself."

"So give me some clues, Mom." Andy said it as gently as he could.

"And deny you all that good self-discovery? I couldn't do that, Andy. Now if you would please pass me the green medicine, I think we should be turning back. We'll have a wonderful spinnaker run home, don't you think?"

Deedee's landing was perfect as always, the bow stopping just a few inches from the dock. Andy had dropped the sails when his mother turned the boat head to the wind. Now he waited patiently for the *Katie* to stop before he moved to the foredeck. It was their ritual, how she'd taught him. He stepped onto the dock and secured the bow line, then helped his mother off the boat.

Oyslebow appeared on cue and drove Deedee to the house in the golf cart while Andy furled the sails and put on the cover. When he finished, he went into the boathouse and flopped into the old leather easy chair, a cast-off from the house that had found a final resting place near the woodworking bench many years ago. Andy felt exhausted, drained, slightly nauseous. He put his head back in the chair and closed his eyes, hoping if he held still the confetti of confusion in his head would settle like the particles in a snow globe, revealing the object.

The fact that only divine intervention could keep him from going on The Race was taking root in his guts like that monster fetus from the movie *Alien*, the one that comes bursting out of the guy's stomach. He knew one of the amazing things about animals, humans included, was how quickly they could adapt in the name of survival. He hated the idea. He didn't want to adapt. He wanted to puke, or scream, or start smashing things.

Something made him open his eyes. He realized in a second that it was the smell of the boathouse, a heady mix of all the paint and varnish that had ever been opened there; all the mahogany, cedar, and teak that had ever been milled; all the marlin that had ever been cut; all the nylon and Dacron ends that had ever been burned; and the funky odor of saltwater organisms in concert with pilings and the stuff of boats.

It reminded him of the only time he'd ever gotten Oyslebow really furious at him. Oyslebow had spent weeks taking a treasured antique lapstrake dinghy down to the wood and building up new coats of varnish. He had just finished coat number five or six, whatever, when Andy, age twelve, had rushed into the boathouse and flipped on the big band saw to cut something. That was against the rules to begin with. The old saw always gave a jerk when it started up, enough to send tremors into the overhead and shake loose a light rain of dust that settled in a uniform pattern all over the glistening mirror coat of wet varnish that had just been applied to the dinghy. He ran into Oyslebow as he left the boathouse, cut stick in hand. He might as well have been clutching a smoking gun. Under Oyslebow's close supervision, Andy had sanded for two weeks to undo the damage. His fingertips were chafed raw and bleeding long before he finished.

In the rafters above him he spotted his grandfather's old shell stored forever along with a wooden canoe, some paddles, and other gear. Light slanted in through a murky window high on one wall. Against another wall was the old Elco electric launch, another of his grandfather's boats that hadn't been in the water since he died. Still in good shape. He could remember a couple afternoon cruises on the Elco, boring afternoons for a kid, with Grandpa playing chess with some dorky friend of his, plodding along at four knots. Beside it was the Penguin his mother used to race, with him as crew. How she'd wanted him to continue as skipper, but no way, not interested, more important shit to do, whatever.

As he closed his eyes again, a tear rolled down his face.

When he heard the golf cart squeak to a stop outside, he jumped up and walked quickly over to the Elco, a good dark space for recovering composure. Ossie came in and walked over to the bench before he saw Andy.

"Your mother tells me you've got quite an adventure ahead."

Andy turned to look at the old man.

"That would seem to be the case."

"Won't be that bad. S'jus sailing."

Andy took a few steps toward the bench where Ossie was fussing with a carburetor from an old launch.

"Let me ask you something. I can't think of anything I'd rather do less . . . except maybe go to prison. Yet my mother assured me I was going to love it. Now why would she say that, Ossie? Why would she say that?"

Ossie had the carburetor in a metal pan and was brushing it with gasoline, peering at it through little reading glasses as he worked. He kept brushing as he spoke.

"Guess she has her reasons."

Andy spun on one foot, suddenly furious, his temper flaring. He walked a few steps toward the Elco thinking it was ever thus, nothing but bullshit from old Ossie when it came to the family crap, goddammit and son of a bitch! He spun again and walked toward Ossie, ready to do battle with the old man for the first time in his life. He stuck his jaw out and flung the words at Ossie, practically shouting as he finished.

"You guess she has her reasons?? Just what the fuck does that mean Ossie, goddammit . . . !"

Ossie dropped the brush and looked at Andy for a long moment over his glasses.

"She has good reasons, Andy. Damn good." Ossie picked up a rag and began wiping his hands as he walked out of the boathouse.

Andy stared after him. Finally the old man had told him something. He had no idea what, but it was a breakthrough of sorts.

VII

ODD MAN

The idea of having the team spend a couple weeks on Hurricane Island, one of the Outward Bound School sites, was Jan Sargent's. For all his gung-ho affect with the media, Sargent had the goods. You don't win America's Cups and Olympic medals with media affect. That helps; but before the media buys into your act, no matter how entertaining it might be, you have to win a few biggies. It was to Sargent's credit that he could put together an engaging media game in addition to the impressive record he had compiled. And now he had organized this Outward Bound School session with the crew.

A friend of an old friend of Sargent's had apparently suffered the incredibly bad luck of having three ships torpedoed out from under him during World War II. The first two times he found himself in a lifeboat, he noticed the people who didn't make it had just curled up in a wet corner of the boat and quit. So when he ended up in a lifeboat the third time, he quickly removed the plugs and threw them over the side before anyone got wise to what he was doing. It wasn't until after they had exited the mess of burning debris that the sailors in the boat realized they were ankle deep in water. You better start bailing, Sargent's old friend's friend told them: everyone. That time, everyone made it, and the Outward Bound brand of teamwork was born.

Andy had tried to digest all this like a good camper, but it sounded inane to him. Infantile. Like the rap of some inspirational speaker you were meant to buy into. Get the book and the video. Improve your life. Evangelize. Not Andy's cup of tea. In fact the whole thing was a pain in the ass. Up at five thirty, roll out of bed into a two-and-a-half-mile run around the island, and oh yeah, wear your bathing suit because the run ends at a small cove and you will be expected to swim to the other side. The swim was well under a minute, but this was Maine, where the water is goddamn cold enough to stop your freaking heart and make you unable to breathe. At six o'clock in the morning.

Then breakfast, and a morning session on the various challenging obstacles Outward Bound had built in the woods, like slippery, sixty-foot logs with the bark removed, suspended twenty feet up to walk along. You're clipped to an overhead wire. But still, a fall is uncomfortable, not to mention humiliating as you dangle there in the air with the harness crunching your crotch. Then lunch, and off to the mini mountain of granite boulders you're meant to scale. Every other day it's into the pulling lifeboats, old thirty-foot wooden scows that weigh a ton.

Everything was competitive of course, which ran against the Outward Bound philosophy that the more capable "students" were meant to help the less capable get through. "Everyone makes it" was the Outward Bound unofficial motto. As Sargent had said, better get used to that idea. He had a point. More than one round-the-world race boat had come back missing a crewman. And it would never be more competitive than the afternoons when they would race the Rhodes 19s that Outward Bound owned, and that Sargent had asked (paid) them to get in shape. Then dinner, and what? — is Jan gonna read inspirational bedtime stories? Andy wouldn't have been surprised.

This was just the beginning. Day two of fourteen, nothing compared to the twenty to thirty days it would take to cross a 6,000-mile expanse of open water. Day two and already this was a serious drag. Andy's prison term had begun. It was even on an island, like Alcatraz. How fitting.

Andy checked his watch and realized it was time for the press conference Sargent had called. No way to get out of it. So he walked over to where the media was set up in front of the main building, a rustic, hand-built log building of course. The rest of the "boys," as Sargent called them, were already there looking proper in clean team shorts and T-shirts. Andy realized he hadn't changed. The beet juice from yesterday's lunch was brilliant on his khaki shorts, right above the *All American* logo. So be it. He stepped onto the end of the crew lineup.

The presenter started with Sargent, who was his usual smooth self, talking about the race, 30,000 miles in nine months with freeze-dried food, four-on, four-off, and all that. Then he was plugging Moss Optical like a good employee, and managing to throw in a few impressive stats about himself without seeming like an egomaniac. Then it was crew time. Sargent had instructed everyone to say his name and one fact the way the starting teams did during televised NFL games. Sargent would then add another comment. Andy figured he'd better listen. He hadn't gotten any of their names, this group of strangers he was meant to go to hell with.

The routine started from the end opposite to where Andy was, giving him time to come up with some dumb fact about himself.

"Stu Samuels, born a Prisoner of Mother England, retired."

"Stu may be our oldest guy," Jan said, "but his bronze medal in the Finn class — for America — wasn't that long ago, was it Stu?"

"Who can remember." Stu smiled.

Stu had set the aw-shucks tone.

"Joe Dugan, sawbones. Ithaca, New York."

"Joe's an emergency paramedic," Jan said. "For me, if it's an MD or Joe, I'll take Joe every time. Don't leave the dock without a doc. Joe's also a veteran. He did the last race."

"Don't tell 'em where we finished," Joe said.

Unlike the rest of the guys, who looked a little rough-cut, Roger Davis had a more polished, Hollywood look.

"RD here. Female specialist."

The boys chuckled.

"Roger Davis," Jan said. "RD is also our sail designer and on board sailmaker. He's another veteran."

"RD . . . " — it was the presenter — "can you elaborate about your female specialty?"

"Someone has to do it . . . " Davis shrugged and got another round of chuckles.

"It is an important role," Sargent said, not wanting to let a good thread drop. He knew what they would run on evening television. "We'll be stopping in seven different ports. Knowing as much as possible about the nature of the women in these foreign ports is very important," Sargent said with a poker face. "We could be at their mercy. RD has done a lot of selfless research." The presenter loved it.

"Who's that tight end next to you?"

"Richard Crouse. Maintenance." Richard did look like a tight end, well over six feet, but lean and powerful. He was a rower, meaning he was a serious guy. Andy knew about Crouse. He had two Olympic medals, pairs with cox, probably the most difficult classification in a killer sport. Impressive.

"Everyone helps with the boat," Sargent said, "but Richard is in charge. He knows where all the bugs live."

"And what kills 'em . . . Larry Kolegeri, that's with one ell, grinder, Knoxville, Tennessee."

"Hold on . . . linebacker, New York Jets, 1995?" the presenter asked.

"That's me."

"Didn't know you sailed."

"He doesn't." It was Sargent getting the laugh this

time. "Actually Larry was one of the grinders on the last Cup I won. That's how he learned to sail."

"Caskie Kolegeri, Larry's brother, also a grinder, also one ell."

"Twins! Identical."

"We don't like to admit it." Another chuckle.

"You also play some ball?"

"Just college. The NFL wasn't big enough for both of us. If we got on different teams we were both gonna die."

"Caskie is a sailor," Sargent said. "He's been Stu's trial mate in the Finn for many years. Won a few cups himself along the way."

"Eric Menici, I'll be doing the video in my spare time."

"Eric's a sailor first. Done well in the foiling Moths. Has to be that way," Sargent said. "No room for riders on this little trip. But he's also good with the camera."

"Anybody who can make Jan look good has to be good," Larry chimed in.

Sargent's smile indicated he'd get even.

"Dave Zimmer, head trimmer."

"Dave is our go-fast guy," Sargent said. "We don't change a sail without running it by Dave — and RD — even when they're asleep."

"We get to sleep?" Dave asked.

"Dave had to put an addition on his house for his one design trophies," Sargent added. "A small addition."

"Peter Dimaris, navigator."

"This will be Peter's third race," Sargent said, "and he hasn't been lost yet."

"Actually," Peter began . . .

"Never mind . . . " Sargent cut him off.

"Dick Hooper, sailor, Kiwi born, but American raised, and I think what Peter was going to mention was that night in Manhattan when it took us two hours to find our car at three a.m."

"Alcohol was involved. Teddy Boswick, also Kiwi born, but a longtime citizen, and I can attest to the fact that we were definitely lost."

"And last but not least . . . "

"I'm Andy Thomas, in charge of naps."

"Maps?"

"Naps, N, as in never."

"Good old MT," someone said at the other end of the line, loud enough to carry.

"Napping is important," Sargent said, "and we've got the right guy in charge. Andy is a vice president at Moss, our sponsor, and I'm told he can sail. We'll find out to-morrow when we have our first boat race."

The presenter was putting a closer on it, but Andy's attention had wandered. He was wondering who had said "MT," and what it meant. MT? Empty? Map technician? Mother Theresa? Me too? He didn't like the sound of it.

"We'll be going off to the boulder course," Sargent said to the group. "'Boulder Problems' they call it, and I've invited the film crew along. They should get some good stuff."

To a climber, the Outward Bound boulder course was a chuckle. But for those who had never thought of a half-inch irregular niche on a rock face as a large foothold one might be grateful to come across, the sixty-foot wall of granite was formidable. The plan was to pair off. One partner minded the safety line clipped to a harness worn by the climber, while the climber tried to find his way up the face, niche by niche. Except for RD, who was an accomplished amateur, none of the boys had any experience. It was slow going. A couple of the Outward Bound instructors were there to remind everyone of the safety rules and offer advice. Andy had ended up with Larry Kolegeri tending his line, which went from his harness to a block anchored at the top, and down to Larry on the ground. That was good. The former NFL linebacker had twenty to thirty pounds on him, and most of that was still muscle.

Two climbers at a time attacked the wall. Caskie, the other twin, another heavy guy, was on his left. Lighter and more agile, Andy found himself doing surprisingly well, finding little toe- and finger-holds to move himself up the wall a few inches at a time. He made the mistake of taking a look over his shoulder when he was halfway up and almost lost it. Thirty feet down looked like a bloody mile. It wasn't the same as being up the mast in a nice, secure chair. Landing on rocks would be a little more painful than landing in the water.

Andy cursed silently that he found himself halfway up some stupid rock wall on an island in freaking Maine. His fingertips were already burning. He knew Michell would get a laugh out of this. Creep. He looked up and found himself staring into a camera lens. Of course. Shoot the Moss guy. Christ! He rested, put his forehead against the cold granite while the rest of him was fastened to the rock by the ends of three fingers and a couple toes. There wasn't much to do but go up unless he wanted to just say screw it and hope Larry had a grip on the safety rope. No thanks. He kept on.

At around the fifty-foot mark, there was a decent ledge to stand on, maybe three inches wide and a couple feet long. Above him, the rock was flat and shiny in the late-morning sun. Not an irregularity to be seen. He looked up. He could see RD's face over the edge of the top. "Okay, here's the deal, MT," RD said. "Look to your right and you'll see a red hunk of half-inch rope dangling down with knots in it. It's about a foot or two beyond your reach, so you'll have to make this little leap of faith. Once you grab the red line, you'll find another little ledge under your feet, and you'll have easy access to the top. So let's go. Go for it."

Andy looked at the rock a few inches from his face. A leap of faith. He wanted to laugh, he really did. It was all safe. Larry was down there on the job. If he missed, he'd just be dangling up there until Larry gave him a safe ride to the bottom. But it was still terrifying. The backs of his knees were tingling. He wanted to pee. What in hell was he doing on this goddamn rock. He thought about Deedee, immovable in her conviction that he had to go on this race. And Ossie, what the hell had he meant by saying she had damn good reasons? Goddamn Ossie. Goddamn Mitchell. Goddamn everybody. He needed a time-out with Jeff, have a look at that redhead with the scarf a mile away. With him gone from work, he wondered who Gloria was abusing. How could you not like Gloria? Again, he had to laugh.

"Shake a leg, MT, no napping." It was RD, getting a laugh from the boys. Andy looked up, saw RD getting a big kick out of this, and exchanging a look with someone on the ground. Jackass, Andy thought, as he left the ledge and lunged to his right, never taking his eyes off the red rope that danced out of reach just as his fingers were about to close on it.

Andy free fell ten feet, enough to make him feel certain that something had gone very wrong. Christ . . . Then sudden resistance, the harness cutting into his shoulders, his helmet connecting with a solid crunch to the rock as he swayed into the wall. He was stunned with fright, unable to breathe for a moment, like diving into Maine water. He was moving, being lowered down, slowly. He used his hands to keep his body off the wall. When his feet touched the ground, his legs felt useless. He collapsed on the ground. He was also just about frozen with anger. He knew he would have had the rope if someone hadn't moved it. If RD hadn't moved it.

One of the Outward Bound instructors was helping him up and unbuckling his harness, asking if he was okay, suggesting a bandage or two for the bloody scrapes on his knees and elbows. Andy shrugged him off. Larry was a few feet away, looking at him with just the hint of a grin.

"Okay?" Larry asked.

Andy looked at him. "I think it's your turn on the wall."

"Lunchtime!" It was Sargent, who'd witnessed the whole thing, deciding that was enough boulder problems for one day.

"Next time," Andy said to Larry, who shrugged.

Andy was a little late for lunch. Joe Dugan had insisted on washing Andy's scrapes and bruises and applying some bandages. Part of Sargent's deal with Outward Bound was for their staff to provide meals for the boys. Healthy stuff for a crew in training. When Andy walked into the dining room, it had already started.

"Hey, what the hell, no cheesbourger!" It was Larry doing his best Bronx brogue. "Hey Dave, you get cheesbourger? They don't got no cheesbourger."

Dave Zimmer: "I got the last one."

Larry: "You're kiddin' me, Dave, right? You gonna share?"

Andy grabbed a tray, took a bowl of mixed fruit, a couple glops of yogurt, a dish of coleslaw, added a ham-and-cheese sandwich, and poured himself a large cup of club soda. Joe was behind him. They were the only two in line. The rest of the boys were already at tables.

Andy headed for an empty seat where Peter Damaris and Dick Hooper were eating. His path took him by the table where RD was sitting. He stopped, waited until RD looked up.

"Whoa, look at those bandages. Anything broken?" RD asked with a grin.

"I got a question," Andy said.

"My pleasure," RD said. Conversation slowly stopped. It was real quiet in the dining room.

"During introductions, I heard you call me MT, pretty sure it was your voice. I wondered what that meant."

"What did you think it meant?"

"Well, I thought Macho Toughguy was one possibility." Andy postured. "Or maybe Meanass Thug. I thought that was cool."

"Aww, no, none of those. Sorry to disappoint."

"Then Mitch Thomas occurred to me, MT, but that's

definitely not me. So what did you have in mind?"

RD smiled again, enjoying the moment. "Meal Ticket, man. You're our meal ticket. That's what MT means — to me at least. I don't want to speak for the boys . . . " A little chuckle went around the room.

"Ohhhh, right, now I get it." Andy laughed. "That's pretty funny. Very funny, actually. Well shit man, if it's a meal you're after . . . " Very calmly, Andy dropped his hands, emptying the contents of his tray on RD's face, chest, and lap. RD jerked away when the combination of fruit, coleslaw, yogurt, and the pint of cold club soda hit him, causing him to fall over backward in his chair, landing with a *crack*! on the floor. Andy shook his tray, making sure nothing was left.

RD lay there for a moment, then slowly got up, being careful not to slip in the mess of food. He stood, brushing off the big pieces clinging to his shirt. Then he took a step toward Andy with fists clenched by his side. No one else in the dining room moved except Joe Dugan, who'd been behind Andy with his tray, which he slid onto a table as he quickly stepped between Andy and RD.

"Oh no," Dugan said to RD, getting in the bigger man's face. "All's fair. Right? All is fair!"

RD glared at Dugan.

"Am I right?" Dugan glared at RD, then panned the room, addressing each sailor with his eyes. "I'm talking love and war here boys, and I'm right, am I not? All . . . is . . . fair."

One after the other, the boys nodded.

"Right," RD said quietly, as he turned and walked slowly out of the lunchroom, heading for the showers.

VIII

SPIN MOVE

Andy, known as "GatherNoMoss" to his online astronomer buddies, was bent over his laptop in his house on Long Island.

Starry: This could be it, I'm not kidding.

GatherNoMoss: Not convinced.

Starry: Come on man, I know you are a believer. With a grandfather like yours. He knew. That's why he built that incredible lens . . . him and the elves. Man I wish he could see this. Here they come baby! The freaking elves are on their way.

GatherNoMoss: He would dig it.

Starry: How long have we been tracking this thing? Three days? I'm sure it has entered the atmosphere. It's gone now. Watch for stories.

Andy signed off, pulled on an old woolen baseball

cap backward, and moved to the telescope, an impressive-looking developmental model Jeff had designed. The telescope was like a small observatory that took up a full third of the large, modern living room sided with glass on three sides, offering views of the woods that were spooky at night. Right then a couple deer could be seen at the edge of the woods, staring in. The telescope Jeff had named the Moss Black Hole 949 was mounted on an impressive steel framework anchored in several tons of concrete beneath the floor. A panel in the roof opened remotely when the machine was activated.

Andy seated himself in the chaise that was custom-shaped to his body. He was quickly engaged. His whole being seemed to be sucked into the silent black void he loved. It had been ever thus since his grandfather had put the old (even then) baseball cap on him and seated him in the telescope chair in his lab. How old had he been, four? Old Randolph Moss had known how to capture the attention of a rowdy four-year-old. He had the big lens focused on the Orion Nebula (Messier 42), the showiest known bunch of burning gasses in the universe.

No doubt the astronomy gene was there in Andy, just awaiting the dramatic, seminal moment when it encountered its destiny. But credit the Orion Nebula for providing the perfect come-on, the hot-fudge sauce for the vanilla ice cream. The nebula was the ultimate color extravaganza, stretching across the universe thirty to forty light years in diameter, reduced to the size of a donut after its journey of 1,344 light years at roughly seven million miles per hour to Randolph Moss's amazing telescope and into Andy's mind.

Somehow, at age four, Andy had gotten it. This was not television. He'd simply gotten the whole amazing, mind-blowing reality of it. Randolph hadn't tried to explain it to a four-year-old. His first goal had been to entertain his grandson. He was good at that. Andy got along better with him than anyone. To be fair, Randolph had thought it might take, or wondered if it would, hoped it would. He'd had Andy in the chair before and there had been nothing. The boy was only four years old. Be patient. Randolph was smart enough not to expect much.

The old man kept trying because he was a scientist, and because he knew he'd been born with a very special strain of something strange and mysterious running through his brain. It would be remarkable if it were passed on. His son hadn't gotten it. He had been a classic second-generation knucklehead with nothing but booze and women on his mind. He'd killed himself in a car before he turned thirty. Whatever it was had taken a different, less productive turn with his daughter Deedee. Or so he thought. Women, with Randolph, didn't really count. Andy was his only grandchild, his last hope.

In that moment when Andy looked into the eyepiece and witnessed the incredible presence of the Orion Nebula, that otherworldly display of supernatural power and Hollywood special effects in a part of the universe so far away most people didn't have the capacity to even imagine it, Andy changed. His whole being had experienced an instant epiphany. His physical self had somehow reset itself, and his mind had been suddenly able to focus for the first time ever. For a kid whose attention span had been around five seconds on a good day, Andy had sat

rooted to the chair for fifteen minutes, totally mesmerized by the Orion Nebula — what it was and where it was.
When he dragged himself out of the chair, the boy had
seemed dumbstruck, wobble-legged. The old man had
been close to tears. He knew immediately that a connection had been made. He felt it. So did Deedee the minute
she saw Andy. Mitchell was unaware of any changes in the
boy. Deedee knew better than to try and explain it to him.

Andy never just sat in the chair of a telescope. He instantly became part of the state-of-the-art optical marvel;
the missing piece. This night at the Moss Black Hole 949,
Andy was motionless except for the thumb of one hand
that was barely moving the fine focus lever. He could hear
his heart beating, providing an outer-spacial soundtrack he
rather liked. It went well with the deepest sound of silence.

He jumped a mile when his two black labs, both
asleep on the couch, woke up barking and scrambled for
the door. Andy caught his breath and cursed. It was Isha,
making a typical high-velocity entrance behind a shield
of shopping bags, oblivious, like any certifiable narcissist,
to what anyone else in the world might be doing.

"My God you can't believe the traffic! Turns out
there was a wreck, bodies, really, bodies, two ambulanc-
es, everything down to one lane. God I hate the traffic,
and people are so stupid, going even slower to gawk at
the mess, all the glass, probably blood although I couldn't
see any, and nothing on the radio, I mean boring, it's so
boring on the road, but hey, here I am, and here we are so
why worry?"

Despite his annoyance at the disturbance, Andy was
amused. What a package, he thought, half-listening to

Isha's ramble, mostly just taking it all in: the choreography, the flash costume, the body, the face, the hair piled up but coming undone in that signature way she liked it, the pouty mouth, the so-very-done-up-eyes with the rad lashes, and the blazing red nails, all right out of a product commercial. He had to admit it wasn't bad, not at all bad. He felt the familiar lust stirring. Thoughts about that evening's date with the Universe were fading.

He went to Isha, gave her a warm-hearted hug. She responded. That was encouraging. He let one hand drop on to that wonderful rise of supple flesh around the hip, and kissed her. It was very good, her kissing back — more encouragement — but it was short-lived. With what athletes who play contact sports call the spin move, Isha twirled away, talking a sudden blue streak about something, a type of behavior that was getting downright annoying and all too goddamn frequent. I mean what about this desire thing, are we supposed to ignore it? Well let me tell you something: it can't be ignored! That sounded pretty good, pretty intense. Andy thought he'd have to try it on her. But not now. She had the floor, as usual.

"Later, Andy, later. Don't you get it? How many times do I have to explain it, that I'm in out-and-about mode, ready for *Women's Wear Daily* to come along, lookin' good, out there, right there, and I'll tell you, there's too much work involved to mess it all up, you know? Later I'll remove . . . everything . . . except my nails, get into the tub, put on my scrubs, those silk ones you like, and be ready for Freddie if you know what I mean . . . capiche?"

Again the choreography was polished. Isha's little dance ended up with her face an inch from Andy's, their bodies just barely touching, with the definite message being sent that this was as close as it would get for the time being. Another spin move. "Besides, you have so much to tell me, like about Outward Bang or whatever. What happened up there in cold old Maine?" She fell into the sofa in polished disarray, giving the floor to Andy.

Andy sat across from her and gave her the two-minute version, the obstacle courses, the boulder climbing, and focused on the sailing, where he had surprised himself and everyone else by being the dominant skipper in the light wind that had prevailed for most of the two weeks the crew had been on the island. "It was odd," he told Isha, who had gone into a rare listening mode, "I hadn't sailed competitively since college, where I did pretty well. But the minute I got into one of those Rhodes 19s — they are kind of a heavy, all-purpose day sailor . . .

"I know the boats," Isha said.

" . . . the minute I took the helm it was like I was back at URI, until I got kicked out. The damned heavy old clunker came alive. My feel was there, like it never left. I was reading the wind, two fingers featherlight on the tiller. I freaking killed them. Okay, I didn't kill them. But there are at least two Olympic medalists on the crew. Okay, so they won their medals a few games ago, and I didn't beat them by much, but hey, this wasn't horseshoes. They were cool, but you could tell they got a little annoyed, suggested we change boats. It didn't matter. I've always been a good starter, and when it's light you know how heavily that counts. And most of the time I called the shifts. Unreal. It really was unreal. Sargent said when anyone else asked me what my job was on the boat I could tell them, 'driver.'"

Andy's laugh reeked of sarcasm. "That's exactly what I want to be, a driver on a goddamn race boat. Christ . . . "

"Really, I have to say in just two weeks you look better," Isha said. "More muscley. I think you might have lost a few pounds. And less drinking. More of a round-the-world sailor boy."

"That's me, that is me . . . " Andy trailed off.

Isha flashed him a dazzling smile, just in case *Women's Wear Daily* photographers were sniping from the woods with their long lenses, Andy thought.

"How was Outward Bang?" Andy said. "It was a pain in the ass. Up at six for a run, plunging into water cold enough to make polar bears refuse, nutritious diet meaning boring food, damn little to drink, no sex . . . pretty much a prison situation."

"Oh, I hear there's a lot of sex in prison."

Andy said nothing. He got up and went to the bar.

"Want something?"

"My martini, please."

"You mean a glass of gin?"

"That's my martini."

He fixed her drink, poured a shot of Zafra 30 rum on ice for himself and sat back down, watched her have a sip of the gin. More choreography. Was there anything this babe did that wasn't a studied routine? He wondered how much time in her life had been spent in front of mirrors. He suddenly wished she were a thousand or so light years away so he could study her with the telescope. That would be fun research. Isha, a new star. Whoa, wait a minute, this was different. He was thinking. He'd just been taking it as it came, just grooving the package, happy with the eye candy, and the all-too-occasional, usually too-rushed drama in the sheets. He hadn't actually thought much about the situation before. Just had another drink.

Isha caught the vibe like it was a fire call. Andy quiet. Thinking. Bad. No matter what he's thinking about, bad. She put her drink down, sidled over to his chair like Cyd Charisse in *Silk Stockings*, and sat with care in his lap so she wouldn't spill his drink on her dress. She got a little pouty, stuck her hand inside his shirt. She took off his wool baseball cap with the other hand.

"I know, your grandfather gave it to you." She put it on, turned the brim sideways and laughed. "I bet I look better in it than you."

Then she kissed Andy, a sweet kiss. Andy felt the little electric shock caused by the surprising contact of tongues. She pulled back. "I'm gonna get ready," she said. "More later. Promise." She got up, grabbed the shopping bags, and headed for her green rooms.

Andy got up, shaking his head, poured himself a touch more Zafra 30, and strolled around the room of this ultra house, his brochure-worthy bachelor digs, causing the dogs to look up expectantly. Zoomer, the younger one, got up and came over, nudging his head against Andy's leg. Andy squatted down and rubbed Zoomer's head the way he liked it. Then he laughed out loud and just about fell over because he had just mentally compared Zoomer with Isha. He laughed again. This time he did fall over, just because it felt so good. Zoomer instantly started licking Andy's neck and cheek.

"No tongues, Zoomer," Andy said, springing up. Zoomer went back and jumped up on the couch.

Andy kept cruising, and it was like he was seeing his stuff for the first time. What a freaking collection, he thought. Several exercise machines that had rarely been used. The classic *Pong* set, the first video game, the large commercial version. The major-league-quality first-baseman's mitt, the Wayne Gretzky autographed hockey stick. The *Pac-Man* table that took quarters. The set of Ping irons, still unwrapped, had to have 'em; the eight-foot, radio-controlled J-boat he'd raced twice, now mounted on a wall rack that allowed it to heel just enough so its ten-foot mast missed the ceiling, and causing gravity to shape the sails; the collection of ships' clocks on the bookshelf . . . he hadn't wound one in years; several drones, big ones, sitting ominously on another shelf looking like new because they were. All his Nikon bodies and lenses were on another shelf. It went on. Over beside the J-boat was the fifteen-thousand-dollar gym "thing" that had been sold on the back covers of the fancier magazines for a few months until the wealthy sucker market was saturated. The dogs often slept in it.

Andy shook his head, drained the rest of the rum, headed for the shower.

It didn't take him long. Maybe ten, twelve minutes before he was back, putting his watch on as he walked toward the bar for just a little one before they left. And there was Isha, caught in the act like a cat on the kitchen counter eating the salmon. Isha dressed to kill in some fractional black dress. Isha over at Andy's big work table, as it happened. Isha standing there, bent over the table with half a stack of papers and plans in her left hand while her right hand was about to peel off another one from the sheets left on the table. Isha motionless as a stone, hoping she might become invisible, but still managing a little innocent smile.

"Whoa!" Andy said, changing course quickly toward the table, taking the papers out of Isha's hands and scooping them all up. "No worries, I shouldn't have left them out. Too early to talk about it. Top secret, actually, so I hope you'll keep them to yourself. Damn. Pretty nosy there, Isha."

"Oh Andy, come on, it's not like we don't know everything about each other. I came over here looking for my vaporizer and the map caught my eye." Isha had once again turned on the heat. Andy was immune, busy putting maps, plans, and documents back in order.

"So what's 'Mountain View'?"

"Just a little project I've got going. A little project that is gonna be a whammo by the looks. This is the biggest deal I've ever done. It's gonna blow everyone away, Mitchell included. Especially Mitchell," Andy said evenly. He went quiet.

"What?"

"Thinking of Mitchell made me think about the goddamn race. This" — he whacked the stack of papers against the desk — "this is what needs my attention. Not the stupid race, a nine-month isolation 'driving' a race boat, with a satellite phone that might work on occasion my only way to communicate with earth. I might as well go to Sweden and take the sleep cure."

"Oh, I think you can do both."

"The sleep cure and The Race?" Andy laughed as he walked toward the wall safe with the Mountain View project in a manageable stack.

"You know what I mean."

"There might only be one." Andy shut the safe door, spun the dial.

"Really?"

"Yeah, I'm seeing Deedee tomorrow. I don't have a card to play. Maybe I have a piece of one. I dunno. Or maybe I'll find one under her dresser. I better. This really is my last shot."

IX

SCRAP BOOK

Andy's mother had the scrapbooks out. They weren't dusty, like most scrapbooks. They were well-worn from constant scanning. In truth, they needed to be rebound. They were coming apart. Three o'clock on most any afternoon and right here in her bedroom was where you could find Deedee unless some minor crisis had gotten her up. She napped at two, and by three she was waking up by paging through one of half a dozen elegantly bound memory-lane books having to do with what? Better days, Andy guessed. Anything had to be better than his mother's life at the moment. It wasn't like some raging illness had gotten hold of her, or she didn't have enough to eat, heaven forbid. The doctors fussed over her all the time, but Andy swore she wasn't sick, not in the usual sense anyway. She just didn't do anything. The servants ran the house, cooked the meals, dusted the sailing trophies. Deedee just existed. She was still the power. She had the control, the assets, Moss Optics, but power was a word foreign to her. She didn't relate to power. She was smart as hell. Andy knew that. But power?

She had paused on a page that showed a photograph of Andy, age three. Andy glanced at it briefly. Old pictures of himself didn't particularly fascinate him. There he was, another gawky-looking kid and so what, just another grain of sand on the beach. But today his eyes were drawn across the page to the arresting shot of his mother playing tennis. He'd seen it a dozen times, but man, what a shot! The photograph was evidence that his parents would often hire a pro for the day to shoot the family activities, the tennis, the sailing, the cocktail hour with friends. This shot was taken with a long lens from Deedee's opponent's point of view, the shutter having been released a split second after Deedee had smacked a scorcher of a two-handed backhand. The ball was about a foot off the racket, a blur. Both Deedee's feet were off the ground. Her body angle was perfect, with every ounce of her diminutive self coiled into the perfect launchpad for the exact moment when she contacted the ball. Her eyes were still on the racket face where the ball had hit. Her skirt — white of course — swirled with the full-body effort. Her teeth were gritted in a grimace of determination. You could almost hear the solid thwack. That sucker was a put-away, no question about it. Talk about power. So where had all that gone, Andy wondered. And the sailing. He knew how good a sailor she was. You didn't get there without confidence in self, without the power to prevail.

"Pass me that next one, Andy. Number three."

Andy knew number three. He reached into the book-case on the shelf over the head of her bed and pulled it down, the fading number having been imprinted in gold on the navy-blue leather binding. "I wanted you to see the old picture of you and Becky."

Andy groaned. "Mother, sorry, but you show me that one every time I come."

"Well, it's important, dear. Because she is such a wonderful person."

Andy might have ignored it, might have just changed the subject and rolled on like he'd done several times be-fore, but he had to remember why he was here. To find his missing card, the card he could play that would get him out of The Race. It had to be here somewhere. He'd looked under the dresser just for fun. Nothing. Maybe Becky Cotton had it. It was worth having a look.

"That was years ago, Mother. Of course I remember Becky. We had some good times. The Cottons were like relatives. Becky was the girl next door. But that was then. This is now."

"Well you should see her now, Becky. You would if you ever came to the club for dinner with us."

Deedee opened number three and quickly found the page with the amateur snapshot of a girl and a boy around thirteen or fourteen years old standing on the dock, two kids obviously unenthusiastic about having their picture taken. They were standing next to a small sailboat with the mainsail neatly furled, the lines coiled. Perhaps be-cause of his mother's teasing, or because he was desperate, he really looked at the photo this time and suddenly he was back in the sail loft with Becky after that afternoon on the water, the two of them collapsed on a pile of sails feverishly kissing and exploring. Making out, it was called then. Whoa. Andy took a breath, and started laughing.

"What is it?"

"Just a memory." Andy laughed again.

"Good."

Deedee flipped the page. There was Grandfather, also dressed for tennis. No action shots. More like he was dressed for watching tennis after maybe playing one slow, boring set. Randolph was very aware of the camera. He seemed to be restricting himself to what he thought were poses appropriate as head of the family. Deedee and Mitchell were also in this collection of photos, which Andy expected were of the cocktail party because they were also professional. Lovely black-and-white prints. Because the photographer was Art Kane, a genius who did all the Moss advertising work, he couldn't help probing in spite of himself, and Kane had managed to do the impossible: capture telling moments and expressions in such a way that his subjects had to like them. A good trick. Andy was really looking now, after receiving the intense message from Becky, and he found himself being amazed still again by the unusual degree of formality expressed by his parents' generation. They were in their late thirties in these pictures, in their prime, and they came off like old fogies. Stiff. No energy. Proper to a satirical degree. Sometimes he listened to himself talking to his mother and it was more like he was talking to his grandmother.

"I have to say, Mother, these 'family' pictures, or the cocktail party, whatever it is, they have a very . . . formal .

. . feel to them." The critique just popped out. It surprised Andy. He'd stopped asking his mother about the family long ago. It was a dead end. But it occurred to him that maybe this was his card. The other approaches hadn't worked. It was an old approach, but a new time.

"You grandfather had a very strict, old-fashioned sense of propriety," Deedee said, as she reached for the familiar bottle of green medicine that was on her night table. She undid the cap and took a swig, no apologies this time for drinking from the bottle.

Andy about slid off the bed at this straightforward piece of information coming from his mother. It was a bland enough statement about someone, but from her it was remarkable. Could he be feeling the tumblers clicking in this safe he'd been trying to open? He was back on the boulders in Maine, tenuously hanging on with a few fingertips and toes.

"Yeah," Andy said, carefully, so as not to disturb this sudden tiny fissure that had appeared in the impenetrable wall of family folklore. "I certainly got that from him. Then again, I only saw him in his lab, and I was still young when he died."

Deedee was studying the pictures like she'd never seen them before.

"I'd say he did have a sense of superiority about him," Andy ventured, desperate to sustain this frail thread, "the way he ran things. I can see it in these photos. But hey, he deserved it. What he did revolutionized the industry." Andy felt a little awkward, talking too much.

Deedee looked up, then turned to Andy, looked him in the eyes. Right then he knew how her opponent had felt twenty or so years ago just before she'd hammered that backhand that froze him in place. Her eyes had lost their habitual cloudy stare and had come alive. Andy was frightened for a moment. "Randolph didn't think he was better than other people," Deedee said evenly. "His main concern was that other people might not understand he was better than them."

Andy said nothing. That was a lot to digest.

Deedee started coughing. She reached for her medicine, took a swig. The coughing stopped.

Myrtle, the maid, came to the open door and knocked quietly. "The doctor called. He'll be here shortly, ma'am."

"Thank you, Myrtle."

Deedee got up and went into her changing room, shut the door.

Andy got up and stretched, trying to get his bearings, feeling totally off track. Randolph worried other people might not realize he was better than them? Man, what a thing to say, what an attitude . . . Christ, he hadn't even had a chance to talk about The Race, give her the last big pitch, and now the freaking doctor was coming, game over. Damn. Okay, he'd have to force the issue. The doctor could bloody wait.

He'd circled the bed and found himself staring at the bottle of green medicine. He picked it up, idly curious. He unscrewed the cap, had a sniff. Nothing. No odor. He shrugged, decided to take a tiny swig and — what the hell?! He couldn't believe it. All these years? He quickly replaced the cap and reseated himself on the other side of the bed. Just in time, as Deedee came out of her room dressed for the doctor, hair brushed, no makeup as usual.

She sat down in the wing chair across from the foot of the bed, her feet flat on the floor, hands folded in her lap, and looked at him. Andy realized she knew him, knew what was coming. Busted before he even began. Christ. Too bad. He had to get it out.

"Look, Mother, I really need your help. We've talked about this before, and now it's extremely serious, my going on this race, it can't happen, it just can't happen. Okay, I screwed up, I brought it on myself by being drunk, careless, stupid. I was out to get Mitchell and I got him all too good. I'm sorry about that. What really happened is I got myself, and I should pay for that. But soon I'll be able to. I have this very big project going, a big deal, it's gonna make me a ton of money so I can help underwrite the expense of entering this boat. But I can't see this deal through while I'm spending nine months helping sail a boat around the bloody world. I can't. It's one thing or the other, and believe me, it's no contest. You've got to step in for me. You're my last hope. I hate to put you in a spot. I know, I've done it a lot. But this is the last time, I promise."

"I'm told you won the sailing in Maine."

"Yes, that's true, I did."

"I was so proud to hear that, Andy. And you're going to be a driver?"

"Yes, that's what Sargent said. You taught me. But, Mother, I'm twenty-four years old, I'm very committed to this business deal, and while I agree it's great that I have been named a driver — I don't for a minute discount that, that . . . honor — I simply cannot drop out of life for nine months, scuttle my deal . . . I just can't. I can't. No way."

Deedee was sitting very still. She spoke evenly.

"When your grandfather died, my father, he called me in, told me to shut the door. I sat on the bed very much like you are sitting on my bed. I was very excited because I thought he was going to pass on to me what he had. He'd often mentioned it. Not in any serious way, but he'd use old joke lines, say things like 'someday all this will be yours.' It started when I was a kid, when he confided in me about the elves. I was first to know, you know. No one else but me knew for years. 'You'll have what I have,' he'd whisper to me. 'You'll know.' So I believed him. I believed he had the power to do that. And I think he did. I know he did. But he didn't. He called me in. He took my hand, and he said, 'Ahh, Deedee my sweet, if only I could pass on to you what I have. But I can't. Because it wouldn't fit. It's that simple. It wouldn't fit. It just wouldn't fit.'

"That's the last we spoke. He died the next day. He left me the estate, the boats, the company . . . everything. But he wouldn't leave me what he had. He could have, but he didn't. He didn't because he was worried I wouldn't think he was better than me. He had to die making sure of that."

Myrtle appeared with her quietly insistent knock. "The doctor is here, ma'am."

"Thank you, Myrtle."

Deedee stood up carefully, like she always did. The surge of energy was gone. The eyes were flat again, but a touch of the voice was there. "Go on The Race," she said. "It's a miracle it came up. You're right. You made it happen, being drunk, being clever. Being obnoxious. But that makes it special. Very special. You don't know. Go on

The Race. Drive the boat. You'll be fine. Your big deal will wait. There are much bigger deals waiting to happen for you. But first, you must go on this race. You might even win it."

Deedee went off to see her doctor.

Andy flopped on the bed, fighting back tears.

X

40 KNOTS

Andy was standing with the rest of the crew looking at the big computer screen designer Gibb Frey was using to illustrate the points he was making about the sixty-footer he had drawn. Frey might have been everyone's number-one draft pick as a designer, but as a talker this beanpole of a guy with the wire-rimmed glasses had one setting: drone. Andy figured Frey must be a good salesman, having convinced both Mitchell, the owner, and Sargent, the skipper, that a sixty-footer — or technically sixty-three feet and a few inches — was the way of the future. According to Frey, the maxis that had recently ruled The Race were dinosaurs, on their way out. The sixties were the new Formula 1 sleds: fast, efficient, and assuring one bone-shaking, very wild ride for the crew, with occasional terrifying moments.

The Frey 60 was flat-bottomed, as ocean-going monohulls go, with wide hindquarters tapering just a little from the maximum beam to a wide transom. The new look. Or an old look. It reminded Andy of a basic scow, a 100 year-old design, a boat meant for lake or sheltered sailing. A long narrow section extended from the maximum beam forward, and it was very shallow. And flat. The keel cord was amazingly thin, with the bulb fastened amidships. Twin rudders. At first glance the boat looked extremely fast — in flat water. The lack of buoyancy forward was startling. It definitely did not look like a vessel one would chose for crossing oceans. Of course if comfort and safety didn't matter, well, that was something else: call it a Frey 60.

"So, Gibb, what's the top speed for this baby. Can she hit thirty? Maybe thirty-five? More?" It was navigator Peter Dimaris, asking what everyone wanted to know.

"In the right conditions, we're getting indicators from our models and other testing that this boat could hit forty knots," Frey said. There was quite a long pause. The boys waited. "But the crew cannot."

There was silence, then Sargent laughed to break the spell. Forty knots. The boys' feet shuffling around on the concrete floor was the sound of anxiety. Several of them exchanged little grins that were meant to be brave.

"What conditions?" It was Crouse, the Olympic rower.

"You don't want to know," Sargent said. "Am I right, Gibb?"

Frey just smiled. "I know you don't want to hear this," Frey said, "but I have to remind you that statistics prove seventy percent of any ocean race is sailed in light air."

"Thanks. Knowing that should keep us dry when it blows," Stu Samuels said. Nervous laughter.

"Should make for some great pictures," Eric Menici said. More shuffling of feet.

Frey moved on to film clips from previous races. One clip showed a crew duct-taping a large crack in the side of the hull caused by a collision with a whale. The next clip showed a boat hove-to with men overboard working near the transom. Frey was talking about safety. Caskie Kolegeri chimed in.

"This boat of yours will be impervious to whale attacks?"

"No, man," Dick Hooper said. "We're just meant to bring extra duct tape."

The laughter had the sound of anxiety. Whales were one thing. No one mentioned the hundreds of containers lost off ships every year. Many of them sank, but just as many floated around until they fetched up on land somewhere. Hit one of those and you'd need more than duct tape. But talking about them was pointless. They were just there, like deer on country roads.

Frey smiled, focused on the rudder-repair video clip that was still playing. "There will be extra stress on the rudder with the high speeds expected," he said. "Rudder problems are no fun. We're working hard on everything concerned: shape, stock, composition, post, hull reinforcement . . . doing a lot of testing, both theory and with actual rudders we've had made. We've tested how many to destruction, Bradley?" Frey aimed the question at a heavy-set man with a ruddy complexion. "Six as of yesterday," he said.

"Do we have that film?" Frey asked.

Bradley punched a code into the active laptop. Suddenly an image of Niagara Falls burst on the screen in all its gorgeous power, a spectacular sun-drenched drone shot that slowly pushed into, then up, over, and beyond the falls into a section of the Niagara River before the drop. The film cut to a shot inside an enormous tunnel into which a large volume of the river was diverted on a daily schedule. The tunnel ended at a power station. The next shot was of a welded stainless-steel structure built in the tunnel to hold a full-scale hull section containing the rudder. The rudder was submerged into the immense volume of water rushing past at the rate of 63,000 cubic feet per second. The rudder was turned at a good angle of resistance. The disturbance it was causing left a thirty-foot plume of white water.

"We figured why build a test station when Ontario Power built this tunnel in the 1950s," Frey said. "We just had to convince them we knew how to manage what we wanted to do. Luckily the O.P. boss has one of my boats. This immense volume of water is moving at about sixty miles an hour, we figure. A couple weeks in this tunnel, turned at fifteen degrees, tells us a lot about a rudder's strength and endurance."

Andy had to admit it was impressive. Certainly the incredible tunnel, forty-some feet across, funneling all that water down into the hydro-station and turning it into electricity, was impressive. A hundreds-of-millions-of-dollars test station. And legal, in "All-American" parlance, because officially the Niagara River was shared between Canada and the United

States. And the O.P. boss had a Frey boat. What a laugh. How the world works.

Andy's phone vibrated in his pocket. He slipped out of the room to answer. It was Jeff Linn passing on a message from people working on his Mountain View project. Jeff knew about Andy's secret project. He would be very much involved when the time came. But Andy was puzzled.

"Why didn't they call me?"

"Actually, I asked them that," Jeff said. "They said it was safer to put the call through your office phone. It was lunchtime. Gloria was out. I picked up."

Andy left the building, went out and sat in the Porsche and dialed the number Jeff had given him. Soon he was in deep discussion with George Cooper, his lieutenant for Mountain View. The idea that had come to Andy one night when he was staring into space in the chaise of his Moss Black Hole 949 was for a grand hotel complex built around the theme of astronomy. The centerpiece would be a high-end telescope several stages more elaborate than the 949, designed by Jeff, and supervised by professional astronomers. Time at the telescope for hotel guests would be apportioned in half-hour segments. George Cooper had sent new exterior drawings of the expansive campus to Andy's laptop, drawings that showed an interlocking series of low, dark buildings with no hard edges. The outer-spacial landscaping was more like set design, with a moonscape here, Mars around the corner, Saturn looming in the background, and so on. There would be a planetarium. Guest's rooms would be named for galaxies. Live star patterns would be broadcast upon the rooms' ceilings at night. The dining room would feature dishes named for the constellations. Drinks would range from a Black Hole (Diplomático Reserva rum, dark Belgian chocolate, and coffee), to a Silver Moon (Monkey 47 gin, saguaro bitters, and Meyer lemon juice). Details included all exterior doors being equipped with air-lock sound effects. Guests would have to apply months in advance so they could be approved. Children over age six would be admitted only after an interview with a psychologist indicated they would make agreeable guests. Children under ten would eat in a special dining room and attend special programs.

Andy eagerly consumed the new drawings on his laptop. Many of the ideas were his. It was taking shape, and that was very exciting. "This place is gonna make Disneyland look like a Model T Ford," he said to Cooper. "One question about the telescope, is it . . . "

Andy was startled by Mitchell pounding on the car window. Andy rolled it down. Mitchell's normally unpleasant expression was extra cross.

"I can see you don't give a crap about the boat," Mitchell said. "You think we put this little act together for Mr. Frey's ego? You wanted to meet me at the club for dinner? Six o'clock. Be on time. I have an early morning."

Mitchell turned on his heel and walked away.

At quarter to six, Andy walked into the bar at the New York Yacht Club's Harbour Court Station in Newport. It was early. The crowd was thin, no one he knew. Early, because he needed to take the edge off if he were going to survive another goddamn dinner with Mitchell.

But he had to see him. He had to admit, there had been a few moments when the idea of getting away from it all, going to sea for nine months like some shanghaied drunk, had had a lot of appeal. Away. Just freaking away. It didn't matter where. There were days when Andy felt like one of Joseph Conrad's sorry blokes. Life ashore always turned them into drunks and brawlers. At sea they became calm, reasonable men. There were some tough days at sea, a hell of a lot of boring days, and some damn fine days. One could get into the rhythm of it after a while.

"Mr. Moss, what can I get you?"

"Hi, Milton. Tequila, please. Got any of that good stuff on the top shelf?"

"Yes sir." Milton pulled over a ladder and ascended to the top of the middle cabinet above the rows of bottles, opened a door, and extracted a bottle of Milagro Reposado, the one with the blown-glass cactus bud inside it. Even the bottle was a work of art.

"Rocks, extra lime. Can't wait."

Andy took a seat at one of the bar tables where he could see Don Demers's painting of *Bolero*, one of the great old yachts that had raced in the fifties when wealthy owners laid ten-thousand-dollar bets on the table over dinner, when ten thousand was worth around ten times that today. The former owner of this grand house that had become a yacht club had built, owned, and raced *Bolero*. John Nicholas Brown, a man who had inherited a slave-trade fortune. Great philanthropist. Good man by all accounts. His family had started Brown University. Brown had *Bolero* launched in 1949: seventy-three feet of pure naval architectural beauty by Olin Stephens, the great one. Black. Gold cove stripe. *Bolero*, da-da-da-da — da — dunt. And Demers had painted the boat. It was called *Bolero off Bermuda*. Andy had never seen a painting of a yacht in full fly that expressed such power. The club's photographer, Dan Nerney, had provided the image Demers had used. The perspective of *Bolero* blast reaching from the leeward side was from the low angle of a small boat, with this lithesome creation harnessed perfectly to the wind, crew at full attention, solid white spray shooting up from the bow inside the big genoa as the boat lifted above hull speed, tearing past less than a hundred feet away. Nerney had nailed it. Demers's challenge was to capture the moment, enhance the power, and he'd done it. Never mind that the water wasn't exactly the color of the sea off Bermuda. Never mind the lighthouse in the background looked more like Monhegan Island than St. David's. Never mind the main boom was a foot or two too long. The power was there. Those moments when he could lose himself in this painting, Andy could almost hear that eerie sound of a large, proper sailing yacht passing, if one was lucky enough to be close to it; the smooth whoosh of water a well-formed displacement hull creates when it parts the waves. The wind would add a barely discernable top note to the passage, the violins trilling at triple pianissimo.

Milton gently set Andy's Milagro on the table.

There had been several times Andy had driven to the club just to have a few moments with this painting. He thought about offering to buy it one time. But it should stay here. John Brown's boat. John Brown's house. He sipped the ice-cold Milagro. More perfection.

"Andy Moss!"

Two older gentleman he'd seen a dozen times at the club were on him like locusts. They were such habitual flies at the club bar, and with such one-track conversation, they had acquired nicknames: Whit and Bred, after the initial name of the round-the-world race. Andy cursed his bad luck as he watched Bred nod at Milton for their usual.

"So great to have a boat in the race at last, an American boat," Whit said. "When we did the race in eighty-one, called the Whitbread back then, when we did the race with Conny van Rietschoten we got a lot of heat about no U.S.A. boat . . ."

"I mean heat," Bred said.

"What a race, nine months, thirty thousand miles . . ."

"You know we won every leg . . ."

"First to finish . . ."

"First on handicap . . ."

"It was Conny's second win . . ."

"We had the maxi. You know what he said about getting the maxi?"

"'When money is no object, why not?'"

"What a guy . . . when money is no object . . . Ha ha."

"Whoa, here he is, Mitchell Moss, the man of the hour, the man behind the first American boat in The Race."

Andy couldn't ever remember being relieved to see his father arrive, but there he was, an on-time guy, now bearing the full brunt of Whit and Bred's inane conversation. Does this happen to everyone who sails The Race, Andy wondered as he watched the antics of these two aging clowns who had somehow made fortunes in the bond market. He remembered seeing an ESPN T-shirt: "Once you've been touched by the Whitbread, life is never the same." He chuckled to himself as he quickly drained the delicious Milagro that was beginning to put a very agreeable, soft-focus filter on the scene. He caught Milton's eye for a refill, then stopped on the image of *Bolero*, still cutting a swath through the ocean.

Mitchell had quickly dispensed with the old ocean racers and was making for the dining room at a good clip. Andy followed before Whit and Bred had a new chance to attack. He saw Mitch seating himself at "his" table by the window, a great spot overlooking Newport Harbor with the lights on the bridge to Jamestown jutting their familiar bosomy outline into the darkening sky.

Mitchell was already studying the menu as Andy got to the table. He had barely gotten seated when a couple approached and hovered. Friends of Mitch come to heap praise on him for putting a boat in The Race. Another old Whitbread racer whose life had never been the same. His wife was enthusiastic, having long been re-signed to live with the endless reruns of the stories, and having learned to pitch in, add those little details that her mate might have forgotten. But he was launched, and this time Mitchell was a prisoner, literally backed into a corner of the dining room with no place to go, no place to hide. Andy stood by politely, amused by Mitch's dilemma, waiting for the inevitable diversion, the pass-off to him, and here it came, the introduction, my son Andy who will be going on The Race because I'm busy running the company and all that, and Mr. and Mrs. Dougherty — or was it Commodore and Mrs., no matter — saying what a wise decision that was, that The Race was for younger men, then turning to him, mouths agape, so proud to meet one of the crew, how marvelous, what a great experience lies in store for you, what a lucky fellow, my, my, and hullabaloo. Andy worked on preventing his smile from melting.

"Ever cross the equator, son? No? Ah ha, you'll enjoy that little ceremony. Better hide your boots, aha ha ha."

"Now Howard . . . "

"But seriously, rounding Cape Horn, now there's something I'll never forget. Not many of us have done that, you know, on a sailing yacht. It blows a gale down there one day in four you know. You must watch Irving Johnson's film. That will get you ready. But what a magnificent journey, The Race, following the routes of the great explorers, trapped in the doldrums — 'water water everywhere and all the planks did shrink' — ahh, and the roaring forties."

Bless the waiter for arriving with some warm rolls.

"Howard, we really must not interrupt their meal. Come, darling, it's such a pleasure to have met you . . . "

Mitchell's smile was broad for the farewells, and disappeared faster than a thief with a purse. He was taking a bite of a roll by the time Andy got seated. Milton arrived from the bar with the refreshed Milagro.

"How many is that? Two? Three? I thought you were in training."

"Part of training," Andy said, lightly.

"Boat's coming along according to Frey. Damn near done. I plan to go have another look next week. How's the trial horse working out?"

"It's not a sixty, but it's a good trainer. The sixty sure sounds like a handful."

"Sargent sent me some videos. I like the numbered shirts."

"His idea. Everything we do on board is taped. Maneuvers, sail changes, short-handed stuff while one watch is below, moving sails around. Everything. At meetings Sargent runs the video in slow motion and critiques it, rescripts the moves like a football coach. Next time we're better, we cut our time down, improve the safety."

"You're a driver?"

"Seems so."

Mitchell smiled, shook his head. "That's amusing. They're that desperate?"

Andy sipped his drink.

"The reason I wanted to talk is I went to see Mum a few days ago."

"The doctors think it's Epstein–Barr."

"Yeah, I know, but I have to say she doesn't seem that sick to me. Maybe just depressed, I dunno, I'm no doctor, but she can be quite with it at times, you know?"

"Not much of the time."

"If she only did something."

"Don't. Just don't go there."

"Okay, okay, old story, I know, but she went to get dressed for some doctor who was coming to see her and I was just pacing around the room, and for the hell of it I picked up her bottle of green medicine. Just curious, I guess. I smelled it. Nothing. Then I tasted it. It's vodka, vodka with food coloring. Did you know that? Pure vodka! How long has she been doing that?"

"Oh for chrissakes, Andy. Your mother's been an alcoholic for as long as I've known her. You didn't know that? You should. You're following in her footsteps. It's not just vodka. Dr. Marshall prescribes it, puts other stuff in it, says maintaining a certain alcohol level isn't bad for her. Keeps her happy."

"Happy?! Jesus, you think your wife, my mother, is fucking *happy*? Does she look happy to you? Maybe you don't even see her anymore."

"You listen: that side of your mother's life is none of your goddamn business, nor is it for discussion or speculation. Got that?"

Inside, Andy was reeling. He met Mitchell's cold, vicious eyes and held on for as long as he could. They were demonic. They burned. Then he picked up the Milagro, took a generous sip, and gently replaced the glass on the table.

"Enjoy your dinner," he said to Mitch with all the cordiality he could muster. Then Andy got up, calmly pushed in his chair, and left the dining room.

XI

LAUNCH

The band saw woke Andy. He opened his eyes, but
didn't move otherwise. He struggled to get his bearings.
He was on a boat, lying on a narrow bench atop a thin
cushion. He had a moth-eaten lap robe pulled over him.
It was not comfortable, and it also smelled quite musky,
the mix of dust, wood, mildew, and fuel that accumulates
when a boat is on the hard for a long time. His head felt
heavy, the typical morning after too many drinks. He had
to think. Dinner with Mitch, or no dinner actually. What
a louse, Mitch, so casually dismissive of his wife, Andy's
mother. Andy had walked out on him, no hysterics, no
yelling that would have upset the other diners who were
more or less innocent. A smooth move for a change, just
getting up, pushing his chair in to indicate it was termi-
nal, and not a bad exit line: "Enjoy your dinner."

Alone, he could have added, and hope you choke on it, but probably more effective left unsaid. The eyes. He remembered Mitch's eyes and how they burned, mean, vicious eyes out of some bad movie where they had used monster filters on the camera lens. They wouldn't have needed filters if they'd had Mitch. And those eyes again as Andy delivered that "enjoy your dinner" line, those eyes with just that tiny flicker of concern that blipped across the cold landscape of hate. That was a win, wasn't it? Not much of one, but enough to sustain him, enough to buoy up Andy on the rocky, unfamiliar path of confrontation.

Okay, he was in the boat shop, Ossie's shop, having crashed on the big old Elco electric launch that had been parked in there for a decade, maybe two, ever since Randolph, his grandfather, had died. He had ended up on the Elco after hitting a couple bars on Newport's Thames Street just to dim the lights a little more, after eating some fried, greasy junk, after driving like hell to get the last ferry out of New London to Orient Point where he had downed another couple drinks for the ride. After negotiating the back roads to the estate. Those weren't exactly the sharpest memories, although he did remember getting on the ferry because Chris, the deckhand, had recognized his Porsche drifting with tires squealing into the parking lot and had held the gate for him. They were useful facts because it was the only way he could have ended up on the Elco, the autopilot having taken over once again.

His bladder was about to burst. He sat up slowly, stood up and waited for a moment until his gyro stabilized, his hair brushing the canvas overhead. He began looking through the compartments under the benches until he found a container, a very tarnished sterling-silver mint-julip cup with its enamel yacht-club burgee still intact. It was engraved with his grandfather's initials. Perfect.

The band saw was humming away, singing its tune as wood was maneuvered into the blade, reminding Andy why the autopilot had taken him to the shop for the night. Ossie was thirty or forty feet away, engaged in his work. Andy lowered himself carefully over the side of the Elco, wondering how the hell he'd ever climbed up there last night. He carefully retrieved the brimming cup he'd placed on the narrow deck outside the coaming. He walked to where the runabout was moored inside the shed's overhang, emptied the cup into the water, and stuck it in his jacket pocket. He rather liked the cup. No need leaving it on the Elco. He'd polish it.

Andy walked over to the electrical outlets, waiting until the cut Ossie was making was finished, and pulled the plug on the band saw. Ossie froze, looked around, saw the lights were still on, turned, and saw Andy. Then he did something Andy hadn't expected. He laughed. "I'll be damned," the old man said. "What are you doing here."

"I spent the night," Andy said. "On the Elco."

"Of course you did," Ossie said, and laughed again.

"You're in a good mood."

"Why shouldn't I be? I woke up this morning."

Andy laughed. "Me too."

"Plug me in please."

"Nope. Not until we talk."

Something about Andy's tone caused Ossie's shoulders to slump slightly in resignation. He grabbed his coffee and walked to his "office," the old leather easy chairs that had been retired from the house, and put his well-worn boots on a sturdy wooden chest piled with industrial catalogs.

"Buy me a coffee?"

Ossie motioned to the table where the pot was. Andy filled a cup.

"Any food?"

"Knekkebrød in the cabinet."

Andy knew it all too well. Tasteless little crackers tough as wood chips. Norwegian snacks. Better than nothing. Andy grabbed a handful.

"Hurry it up," Ossie said. "I've got stuff to do. If it's about The Race, I can't help you. I told you to go. Just go. It won't kill you. If it does, well, so what?" He chuckled again.

"My mother is an alcoholic." Andy sat in the other leather chair.

"Yes."

"You know?"

"Yeah."

"Jesus, am I the only fool who didn't know this until a week or so ago?"

"Probably."

Andy took a sip of coffee. It was awful, this bitter, murky stuff that Ossie drank. But it was doing the job, softening up the Knekkebrød.

"It's a disease, they tell me," Ossie said. "Okay, but if anyone's got reason, it's your mum. I mean some people just drink, and you wonder why. Not your mum. She don't make a fuss. She's a mannerly alcoholic. She gets around. She lives in a manageable haze."

Since Ossie had turned seventy, Andy couldn't recall ever hearing him say more than three or four words at a time. Especially about family. Now he was pushing ninety. Maybe the endgame was loosening him up a little.

"She's sick I guess."

"Yes she is."

"You know why, what it is?"

"I'm no doctor."

Andy recognized that sound of a door shutting. The band saw was calling, along with the warnings of some age-old confidences Ossie had agreed to keep under penalty of some dire consequence. He'd take what he knew to the grave. That was how he was.

"You coming to the launching? Get my invite?"

"Yeah. Thanks. Naw. Don't travel. Getting from my cabin a hundred yards over here to the shop is adventure enough. Good boat?"

Andy reached in his jacket, pulled some folded eight-by-ten sheets from an inside pocket and handed them to Ossie. "These are crummy copies, but you'll get the idea."

Ossie put on his glasses, unfolded the sheets and studied the drawings. Andy sipped his coffee, feeling the unpleasant heat behind his eyes as sensation returned. Ossie was shaking his head. The beginnings of a smile were rearranging the wrinkles of his weathered face. He was gently shaking his head, chuckling silently. He finally found his voice.

"You're gonna sail this thing round the world, this . . . boat? . . . yeah? I wouldn't sail it across the sound in a breeze. You got no buoyancy forward. You got a submarine here. Really? This is the boat? A sixty-footer that weighs thirty thousand pounds?"

"Gibb Frey's latest."

Ossie chuckled some more. "Hit this thing with a champagne bottle and you'll put a hole in it."

Andy took the papers from Ossie, put them back in his jacket.

"I dunno," Ossie said. "That thing just might kill you."

At the yard, Andy contemplated the actual boat, all red, white, and blue, polished like a new car in a showroom, *All American*, in the travel lift, ready to get wet for the first time. In one of his expansive, younger moments, Ossie had told him that boats have a certain human quality about them in that they are conceived and launched into an adventure full of unknowns. Track the life of most sailboats, he'd said, and you'll find a tale of success and failure, love and abuse, care and neglect, a reflection of those who owned them. Special-purpose boats like *All American* are more akin to the way greyhounds were scientifically bred for speed. There are no placid days ahead for them, no comforting walks with their master in the sun-dappled woods, no treats, no winter evenings curled up by the fire. They race until their legs go. A few are taken in by good-hearted enthusiasts. The rest are put down. So it would be with *All American*, a boat that would be sailed to the edge of destruction for 30,000 miles. Depending on how well it finished, and if it even survived, it might have a second life as a trial horse for a crew awaiting a new boat. Or it would be scrapped.

What an odd thing to do, this race, Andy thought as he studied *All American* looking fast and slick in the travel-lift slings. All the money, all the talent to design and build this thing that would be a throwaway before it was a year old. Compared to dragsters, whose entire career could end in under five seconds, maybe a year wasn't so bad. But still, there was something disturbing about *All American* sitting there looking so bloody gorgeous, knowing it had been born to be abused. He hoped Ossie was wrong, that it wouldn't kill him in the process.

The launching turned out to be a festive occasion with a hundred people in attendance plus reporters and a TV crew, with all the men in blazers and ties, and all the ladies trying to look cheerful in bright summer colors, many with hats. The soundtrack was a riot, with Lester Lanin's society orchestra stomping out its endless medleys of dance music. "Cheek to Cheek," "The Best Things in Life Are Free," "Taking a Chance on Love," "Fly Me to the Moon," "Easy to Love," and a score of other standards all merged together one after the other to the same, identical beat. It was a brilliant thing Lanin had hit on, quite nuts, but also quite infectious. Andy knew it was Deedee's work, getting Lanin. Her generation loved him. She knew him personally, of course. He'd played at her deb party. And there was the old man himself, well over eighty, leading the band with his tarnished trumpet, liberally lasering his classic society smile at the guests. Oddly enough, Lanin was the right choice because it was difficult to be anything but silly happy when Lanin's band played. Some people were actually dancing because they simply couldn't help it. "The moon belongs to everyone" . . . *boom-chik, boom-chik, boom-chik.*

Mitch wasn't dancing. He was making the rounds with his best walking-and-talking routine, shaking hands and exchanging vacuous one-liners with people he thought were important, like any politician. Isha was doing her own dance, prancing about in her own socially scripted world, putting moves on the wealthier men as if she had a list, and maybe she did. Andy wouldn't have put it past her. The wealthier men's wives definitely had a list, a very short one. He was on Isha's list, but he wasn't sure he was on the top anymore. Her snooping around his Mountain View stuff when he was in the shower continued to haunt him. What was that all about? Andy was looking around for Deedee when Joe Dugan grabbed his arm. "The crew is having a little pre-launch get-together," Dugan said. "Come on."

Looking sharp in blazers and *All American* neckties, everyone was there, skipper Jan Sargent included, in a private area to one side of the yard where several carefully arranged containers of gear (one a workshop) insured a degree of privacy. There was a little table in front of Sargent with several bottles of Gosling's Black Seal rum on it. "We've got a problem it's going to take all of us to solve," Sargent was saying. "Some wise guy has opened these bottles, and you know the rule: once a bottle of rum is opened on or near a boat, it has to be finished. Sorry guys, but this requires a team effort." With that Sargent lifted a bottle, took a swig, and passed it on. Soon all the bottles were making the rounds. Someone lit a joint, and soon several of those were also making the rounds.

"I just want to say this is one big-ass day," Sargent said, "our new boat out there about to be launched."

"If they don't drop it," Richard Crouse said.

"Would make good pictures," said Eric Menici.

"We're in pretty good shape," Sargent said. "Now it gets real."

"I'll drink to that," said Teddy Bosworth, raising a bottle of Gosling's.

"I have a toast." It was Dave Zimmer, the head trimmer.

Sargent: "By all means."

"We've never really welcomed Andy Moss, I mean Thomas," Zimmer said, who was starting to slur his words. "Not really. I think we all can agree that we thought he was an asshole at first, the boss's son, a lightweight. But, and I have everyone's nod on this, we've looked him over, and we think he's okay. He's not the boss's son, he's Andy, one of our drivers. So here's to our Andy, asshole no more!"

Bottles and fists were raised. "Asshole no more!" the group growled seriously, several times, sounding a bit like a Kiwi pre-rugby haka.

In the silence that followed, Andy looked around for a bottle, took the one Zimmer was holding, and raised it. "I just want to say," Andy said, "fuck you guys."

The crew cracked up as one, cheering and whistling.

"I told you," Zimmer said to no one in particular.

"All right," Sargent said, "let's go launch this rocket."

The travel lift was in position, ready to lower *All American* into the water with the push of a button. The yard guys had built a handsome set of steps leading to a small platform where the V.I.P.s could wax eloquent about the program, and where Deedee Moss could christen the boat with the breakaway bottle of champagne wrapped in protective netting. Safety first. And there was Deedee on the arm of Sam Cotton, the longtime Moss attorney who had made the initial presentation about this project to the board. Andy greeted them, shook hands with Sam while Deedee straightened her son's tie. Andy thought his mother looked quite happy. Lanin's band was tearing into "Fascinating Rhythm" ("You've got me on the go"), and one could sense Deedee propelled by the familiar sound.

A very striking young woman came up behind Sam and gave him a hug. She was tall, with soft red-blonde hair in a long braid. A few freckles saved her face from perfection. Sam hugged her back, then turned to Andy. "My daughter, Becky, you remember her."

"Hi Andy," Becky Cotton said. "Oh, and this is Robert Hamlin."

Andy was already overstimulated from the gathering at the containers, and the sudden appearance of this old teenage family friend looking so incredibly lovely — so . . . ideal — rendered him speechless for much too long. It was one of those electrifying moments. Becky's "Hi Andy" had stirred a dormant nerve that was still vibrating. Desperate, he glanced at his mother, who gave him the I-told-you-so look in return. And Robert. The boyfriend? "Becky, yes, hi, it's been a while wow, ah, now," he managed to mumble, just this side of incoherence, and much too late he stuck out his hand to Robert, who took it in slightly too manly a grip. "We used to sail together," Andy said to Robert, and immediately thought he could not have said anything more inane. Robert's smile was wan. Becky looked away, then started talking with her father.

Isha picked this moment to interrupt, draping a possessive arm around Andy as she began whining about not being invited to the platform. Mitch barged in and said it was time for Deedee, Sam, and him to get the show started. They headed for the stairs. Andy turned away as Sargent called for the crew to line up under the bow of the yacht. As he did, he cast a look in Becky Cotton's direction, and immediately wished he hadn't. Isha was still clinging to him. The impact of Becky's dismissive smile was staggering.

The boys lined up. The band went quiet. Sam introduced Mitch. Mitch pontificated, praising the round-the-world race, praising the boat, praising the crew, praising Moss Optics, and managing to praise himself. Then Sam introduced Deedee, whose job was to swing the bottle of champagne into the end of the boat's spinnaker pole, which had been rigged and extended within easy reach. Deedee was handed the bottle. She looked distracted. The Lanin band began playing "America the Beautiful," in dance tempo of course. On cue, Deedee swung the bottle . . . and missed. Mitch saved her from flinging herself off the platform. Andy thought he might collapse. The bottle swayed around on its safety line. The crowd held its breath as Deedee pulled herself away from Mitch, grabbed the line, and hauled in the bottle. Andy watched what for him was a replay as his mother grabbed the neck of the bottle in both hands, and with eyes that suddenly blazed, smashed it into a million pieces on the end of the spinnaker pole with a backhand that was definitely not returnable. The applause was deafening.

XII

THAT KISS

Andy was in what passed for sleep on an ocean racer sailing upwind in thirty knots, with the rounded bow section designed primarily for off-the-wind speed slamming into jumbled seas every five seconds or so. The number three genoa, a smaller, tougher heads'l, was up, and a "flattening reef" that just shortened the leech a foot or so had been taken in the mains'l. The traveler had also been raised a foot and the mainsheet eased, which allowed the top of the mains'l to "twist," spilling wind. Even so the heel angle was around fifteen degrees. For cruising, the conditions would have warranted at least one full reef, maybe two, but this was racing.

Andy's bunk, shared with Richard Crouse, a designated driver on the opposite watch, was just forward of the mast. The berths were minimal: eighteen-inch "shelves" built into the hull on each side. Thin mattress pads were stuck with Velcro to the fiberglass. No sheets. And the bunks were "hot," meaning always occupied by someone from one watch or the other. A hunk of micro fleece served as a blanket. After the first day or two, everything was damp, and of all things damp, micro fleece is probably the most agreeable. The shelves were slanted to keep bodies from falling out when the boat was heeled. If the boat wasn't heeled, bodies settled into the V formed by the shelves and the hull. Everyone slept on the high side of the boat to keep weight where it would reduce heel. If the boat was tacked, the off watch sleeping below had to also tack, dragging their half-conscious selves out of their bunks and staggering across the clutter to the bunk on the new high side. But for the moment the course was agreeable, no tacking, and the sleepers were heavily into the rhythm, if one could call it that, of the light, overpowered boat's punishing encounter with open ocean. Talk about David and Goliath. It was like a flyweight taking on a heavyweight in the ring, hoping to dodge the big one that could knock him senseless. Good helming was critical. Luckily Andy and the other designated drivers — Sargent, Stu Samuels the Finn sailor, and Richard Crouse the rower — were all very polished helmsmen. The others drove the boat when the conditions were less challenging.

Andy's ragged sleep this watch was accompanied by a tennis-exchange dream he was having with some unidentified woman. He would hit the ball as hard and as high as he could. His opponent would watch it and wait, like an outfielder positioning herself for the catch, then hit it back as hard and high as she could, and so on. Each hit was in time with the bow slamming into the next set of jumbled seas. Sleeping was exhausting.

A particularly vicious slam of the bow, out of sequence, woke Andy. It happened to the best drivers. The hour-long stint at the wheel in heavy going severely tested their concentration. When the slightest distraction coincided with a roguish sea, the result was a smack side the head that just about stopped the boat and put a big, sudden strain on everything, from mast, rigging, and sails to crew. But it was okay this time. No telling sounds of anything giving way. Andy often saw the boat as a bow, with the mast as the arrow drawn into firing position by the stays. With the backstay tension set around 15,000 pounds, he couldn't imagine what the loading was when the boat ran into a big wave and nearly stopped. He just hoped it wasn't enough to fire the mast arrow through the bottom of the boat. On we go. Andy looked at his watch. He had a few minutes before he had to start dressing for the deck. He shut his eyes and the start of The Race replayed for the hundredth time.

Thousands of people had gathered at the enormous U-shaped race facility on the Southampton docks where all the syndicates were located. Everyone was either buying T-shirts and hats printed with their favorite boat's name and colors, eating junk food, or trying to make their way to the rails of the elevated promenade above the floating docks where the boats were berthed. On board *All American*, Andy was missing. Over the many months since his round-the-world nightmare had begun, he'd finally overcome his inability to deal with the prospect of going. It had taken major effort, but he had settled into the training, listened to Deedee, listened to Ossie, and his success racing the rock stars on the crew in small boats had made a difference. And there had been a couple good weeks in Southampton working on the boat, attending to details, and getting his personal gear organized to fit into the one official bag that had been issued to all hands. There had been some good parties with the crew who had taken him in. That felt pretty good. There'd even been some good times with Isha.

But the day he had to walk down the dock and get on this fragile sports car that was hoping to do an armored vehicle's job of surviving the world's oceans, all the old horrors came rushing back. What was he thinking . . . how could he do this, suspend his life for nine months, put Mountain View on hold? Yeah, Jeff Linn was keeping track of it, but there was so much going on. Andy had suffered a bad setback the day of the start, and taken refuge in one of the containers, actually dozed off on a bunch of sail bags until the silence woke him, or so he thought. It was his name being called that actually brought him around, his name being called in a magical way he'd only heard once before, and that had been recently. "Andy . . . hello . . . Andy?"

He jumped up like he'd been stung, disoriented, looking at his watch, grabbing his bag, saying "Yeah, here I am, hello . . . " as he burst out the door of the container to encounter Becky Cotton standing there like some impossible, angelic hologram. She couldn't be real, but there she was, her presence tweaking every nerve in his body like before, talking a blue streak. "I just wanted to wish you well. I went to the boat and you weren't there. Someone said you might still be here. Dad has told me so much, he wanted me to understand . . . "

Andy was frantic. He was very late. The boat should have left already and in the crowd of tourists he was several minutes away. And here was Becky, being friendly, wanting to talk. How had she found him? What the hell?!

"I am so late. Damn. Sorry. I need to run."

"Wait!" Becky said it quietly, but in a way that would have stopped a train. Andy found himself motionless despite his desperate situation.

"It's just a quick test." With that she walked up to him and kissed him, her lips on his, softly, firmly. It lasted two, maybe three seconds, but time failed. Everything stopped. There was nothing else, just an extraordinary void bubbling with promise, a heart-stopping exchange of electrical charges that made Andy's legs shiver and the bottoms of his feet tingle. Becky pulled away.

"I thought so," she said quietly. "You'd better go."

Andy bolted. "Come to Punta del Este, our first stop, Uruguay, can you?" he hollered over his shoulder as he dove into the crowd.

"I'll try," she said.

Dave Zimmer and Dick Hooper were holding the dock lines, waiting, when Andy raced down the steep gangway to the boat. He jumped on board. Zimmer and Hooper followed. Looking daggers at Andy, Sargent angrily shoved the throttle ahead and *All American* moved quickly away to cheers from the crowd. Andy looked up. There was Becky, having somehow made her way to the rail, just looking at him with a little smile. He smiled back. "Get the number one ready," Sargent said to the boys. "Stow that shit," he barked at Andy. "Get in uniform for chrissakes." Andy dove below, grabbed the number-one genoa, and wrestled it into the hatch so Caskie Kolegeri could get a grip on it.

The start on the Solent was the usual madness, with hundreds of spectator boats raising wakes, or just getting in the way. The wind was moderate, less than ten knots. Course-patrol boats were everywhere, and there were still not enough of them. It was a miracle no one got run down by one of the eight competing yachts. Andy was Sargent's tactician at the start, but he had little to do. Sargent timed it well. He was a great starter. So was his friend and rival Alistair Koonce on the Kiwi entry, *Ram Bunctious*. The same Alistair Koonce who had gotten the whole round-the-world race rolling with his clever, public rap to Mitch Thomas at the New York Yacht Club two years ago, with Andy's drunken comment perfectly icing the deal. Now *All American* and *Ram* were neck and neck at the pin end, with less than ten feet separating the two boats. Their crews worked hard to ignore one another.

Andy had to laugh. So much was invested in the start people would think it was a day race around the buoys, not the beginning of a 6,750-mile leg. But any start is a full macho exercise. *All American* was to leeward, with Sargent taking *Ram* up just a hair as the seconds ticked off — twenty, ten — letting Koonce know he could run him into the pin if he wished; two old pals getting it on, both with broad smiles for the television cameras, and for each other. Andy studied Koonce, seeing that same captivating smile that had Deedee so twitchy that night at the yacht club, the same smile that had caught Mitch so off guard, no easy task, and that had sucked Andy into the worst gaffe of his life, a gaffe that had placed him on this race boat beginning a 30,000-mile marathon across the world's major oceans. Talk about shooting himself in the foot. The gun went off. Koonce cleared the line and immediately tacked away, nearly wiping out a spectator boat that had come in way too close so the women on board could remove their bathing-suit tops and wave them at the sailors leaving for the high seas.

"I beg your pardon, I never promised you a rose garden . . . " The CD player was programmed to come on at full volume thirty minutes before the watch changed.

When Andy had done his six months active duty in the Army, the non-com in charge had woken his men up every day at five a.m. by bouncing a metal trash can across the barracks floor. Lynn Anderson's bouncy bubblegum song from the 1970s was only a marginal improvement, and since it was Larry Kolegeri's idea, and the former New York Jets linebacker was the strongest guy on the boat, no one considered arguing about it. The deal was that whoever got out of his bunk first could turn it off. That was usually Eric Menici, the Black video guy whose nickname on the boat was BN, a caustic but endearing reminder of the old days, one of those politically incorrect slurs that work on close-knit sports teams. It wasn't for public consumption. What happens on the boat stays on the boat, because once cast off, all earthly differences like titles or power better be left on the dock. On board, raw equality rules. All that counts is what you can do. Ask any owner who has had the nerve to expect preferential treatment. There's a captain in charge, but he'd better wash his own coffee cup.

Eric dug his nickname. He appreciated the connection, the love expressed. He also relished the black humor intended. His bunk was next to the communications gear that included the CD player, and he could almost reach the stop button from his bunk, but not quite. Eric usually managed to stop the song before the line played that he really hated: "So smile for a while and let's be jolly."

There was nothing jolly about twelve men trying to live in a space thirty by seventeen feet — thirty feet of living space interrupted by the mast, bunks, the drying locker, a tiny stove and sink, the nav station, and oh yes, the head.

Andy fished in the top of his bag for his toothbrush, grabbed it, and crawled toward the head over the long, narrow "turtles" of extra headsails that were stacked on the floor, reducing headroom to less than five feet. Crawling on all fours was the safest way to get around. The crawling would create thick calluses on his knees and the heels of his hands that would puzzle him when he got ashore after the first leg. Joe Dugan helped him figure it out. "It's the crawling," Joe had slurred after several beers one night. "The crawling." It had made everyone laugh.

Richard Crouse came crawling out of the head as Andy approached. "Sorry, man," Crouse said. "Danger zone." Andy went into the tiny enclosure anyway, wet his brush and quickly took one layer of plaque off his teeth while trying to ignore the smell. There was no mirror. The crew had voted against one. The head was filthy and they'd only been out a week. Soon everyone would be hanging his butt over the side rather than continuing to pretend the amenities of a head existed.

It was wet on deck. Very wet. The racket of sailing in these conditions was intense. The volume of water repeatedly kicked up by the weather bow and landing on the deck sounded like loads of gravel being dumped on a metal plate. One couldn't stand up below even if there had been head room. Andy crawled to the heater locker where crewmen hung their foulies and boots in hopes they would dry a little. They didn't, but it was a nice idea. Andy toasted his arm on the heater. His head made painful contact with the doorframe when the boat slammed into a wave. He grabbed gear, checked to make sure it was his name on the back of the jacket, and crawled back to where the other guys on his watch — Roger Davis, Joe Dugan, Stu Samuels, Caskie Kolegeri — were sitting on the sail turtles, eating. Peter Dimaris, the navigator, and Eric didn't stand watches. They were up all the time, or so it seemed.

"Here ya go mate." It was Teddy Bosworth, today's "cook," handing him a hot bowl of freeze-dried something. "Last of the blueberries, enjoy." Cook was a rotating job because all it took was boiling some water and stirring in packets of freeze-dried whatever. But Bosworth could actually cook. Andy had been lucky to have had dinner at his house. He was also a talker.

"The blueberries really make it edible," Stu Samuels said. "Good idea."

"I got all I thought would last before we left," Bosworth said. "It's about process, cooking. Recipes are for beginners. It's all about what you've got in the fridge. Every meal is a creative exercise. You know *The Iron Chef* on TV? This guy in long robes looking like Japanese royalty comes out into the 'arena kitchen.' A gong sounds, and the prince guy tells three competing chefs to open their baskets and make an appetizer out of crazy shit like some hot peppers, a bag of bean sprouts, a chunk of ginger, and a beef tongue, stuff like that. Great show, because that's what cooking is about."

"Ten minutes! Cut the crap!" It was Sargent poking his head into the companionway and yelling at the new watch. His guys were beat-up, soaked, hungry. The boys below scurried. It took at least ten minutes to wrestle damp gear over damp clothing. Stu Samuels, the watch captain, was talking with Peter at the nav station. They had been making good time, speeding through the always dangerous Bay of Biscay with sails eased a bit, getting a thrilling taste of what *All American* could do when the wind came aft a little, and passing the Faro de Cabo light on Spain's northwest point the previous night. The light had a range of forty miles on a good night, and it had looked bright. Peter was keeping them in close, staying as near the rhumb line to Punta del Este as possible. GPS had them 2,100 miles out of Southampton, off the southern end of Morocco in just a week, not bad. *Ram,* the boat they all cared most about, was further west, going after a storm front Peter and Jan had decided to ignore. The others were scattered around. *All American* was furthest east. That was ocean racing, trying to pick the best weather.

"It's time we tacked," Peter told Stu. "I'll confirm it with Jan when he comes down."

XIII

CLOSE CALL

On deck it was worse than it had sounded below. The conditions caused Andy to contemplate the fragility of this vessel that would be his home for the next nine months. He understood Ossie's disparagement of the boat. The fact that the round-the-world boats were designed and built for speed at the expense of good old sea-keeping ability was bad enough. But one of their worst characteristics was the lack of any protection for the cockpit, where the helmsman worked magic and where the rest of the watch hung out between jobs. Sailboats meant for going offshore have a dodger built over the hatch that deflects the bulk of the spray coming off the bow. A dodger can be elaborate, a virtual "house" open on its stern side, or a solid part of the boat structure that encloses the front end of the cockpit. Minimally, it can be canvas stretched over a collapsible framework. That vital design element was completely missing from the sixty, making them like vintage sports cars or Army Jeeps with their windshields lowered. Why? Because a dodger would slow the boat down! It would create drag, theoretically, costing some minor fraction of a knot of boat speed. It was one of those things that confounded Andy, never more than when, like now, he stepped on deck just in time to get hammered by a large volume of water that had been tossed up by the bow; water that had been blown onto the deck by the wind and had raced unimpeded down the length of the boat until it smacked into the unprotected sailors in the cockpit.

Why! Andy thought with a curse as he got staggered by the hit, and as several ounces of cold water found some space between his foul-weather hood and his cheek and trickled down his chest. If it was the fraction of a knot that concerned teams, why not make it a rule that every boat must have a dodger of a certain dimension? It would be so simple. There were lots of things like that about this race that bothered Andy. His only conclusion was that some twisted macho posturing was at work.

The organizers were proud of the fact that the course selected for The Race followed the tracks of the early explorers. More or less. Because the course also depended upon which cities had anted up, paid the big fee for having the round-the-world show finish a leg in their harbors, bring in crowds to eat in their restaurants, drink in their bars, and stay in their hotels. But okay, the explorer bit sounded good, added historical substance to The Race. Bless those brave guys in their heavy, leaky old scows that were so slow waves broke over their sterns, "pooped" them, often sweeping helmsmen into the seas. But hello, this is the twentieth century. If we can have electronic weather updates every day and the latest in foul-weather gear, then why not a freaking dodger? As Larry Kolegeri was fond of growling after a large chunk of water had pounded the sailors and filled the cockpit, "Aye, laddies, them that died were the lucky ones." If Robert Louis Stevenson's Long John Silver wasn't a macho freak, then who was?

"Big fun, Andy." It was Richard Crouse, ready to give him the wheel. Andy made his way aft, clipped his safety harness to a ring in the deck, and stood beside Crouse for a moment, hanging onto the strong stainless guard that protected the wheel, measuring the seas, getting into the rhythm of it like a relay sprinter preparing to take the baton. "Okay." Both men spoke at once, then chuckled. Andy took the wheel as Crouse let go, transfer complete, smooth as a shark's belly.

They were hard on the wind, Andy's favorite time to drive, usually. But this night was very tricky. The traveler was down halfway to spill wind out of the mainsail even with a full reef taken in the main. And the smaller number-three jib was at work. Andy liked the combination. The boat felt manageable, barely, but that was the idea. Keep it on edge for 30,000 miles, like race cars traveling a fraction of a mile an hour below sliding into the walls on the corners. With the large seas running, momentum was the key. "Higher and faster" was the upwind conundrum. Sail too high and you gained distance but slowed down. Sail too low and you went faster but lost distance. Finding the groove, the maximum speed made good (VMG in computer projection terms) was the answer; that magical, elusive path between high and fast where a particular boat performed at its most efficient. Because they were all different. The instruments were a help if a helmsman could scan sailing angle and boat speed at the same time, but the groove was really about feel. Maintaining it was hard enough in flat water. Add cranky, big seas and gusts at thirty-five to forty and it was tough to find time for the instruments. Sail too low in a blow and the strain on the boat was immense. Too high and the conditions would take over. But get it right and it was immensely satisfying. The groove was one of those really great places to be. On a night like this, staying in it as much as possible was akin to survival. Andy worked it, bow down (lower) in small increments when he could for the speed needed to come back up and take on the next wave. It was subtle stuff. The driver couldn't see the waves very well at night. He had to sense them, hear them. It was a crazy game that also involved those instruments (apparent wind angle, boat speed), sail trim, the condition of the boat and gear, and the wind, with everything in a constant state of flux. Andy remembered having read a bit of wisdom from his all-time primo sailing guru, Buddy Melges, about steering. "The best helmsmen," Melges had said, "are the ones who can keep the most channels open."

It was exhausting on the wheel, but the hour passed quickly. Andy's concentration had been remarkable judging by only one or two whacks from out-of-sequence waves. The limited amount of cursing from the guys in the cockpit who — along with him — were punished by his mistakes was a good sign. Then Stu Samuels was at his elbow, telling him well done, measuring the seas, getting into the rhythm before taking over. "Peter wants us to tack whenever we're ready," Stu said before he took the wheel and zoned out into full focus on his task.

Unlike racing around the buoys, tacking during an ocean race was an event. It didn't happen that often, first of all, and it involved everyone, including those asleep who must move to bunks on the new high side. The tack was called by the tactician — skipper Jan Sargent in this case — and the navigator — Peter Dimaris — and executed by the watch on deck. They could call up others if extra hands were needed, but this night it seemed manageable. Below, Peter woke the off watch and got them ready. On deck, RD would release the active jib sheet, Andy would trim the new sheet, and Caskie Kolegeri would crank the winch. Joe Dugan would be stationed near the mast in case the jib tried to get hung up as it violently luffed around to the other side. Everyone was clipped on in position.

"Ready below?" It was Stuart at the wheel, yelling over wind and water noise.

"Yo."

"Ready on deck?"

"Ready."

"Tacking."

Stuart hesitated, waiting for a little space to open up between waves, found it, turned hard into it, trying his best to sustain as much momentum as possible. The boat responded well. RD eased the old sheet and spun it off the winch drum, then scurried aft to ease the traveler. Andy started with two turns pulling slack out of the new sheet with all his strength. He quickly took a third and fourth wrap and pulled hard as Caskie cranked the jib home. As expected, a wave smacked *All American* on the new weather bow before it had game on, giving the boat a twenty-five-degree knock for a long moment. Everyone hung on. But light as she was, acceleration was quick, and very soon Stuart had her coming up to speed on the new tack. Andy had Caskie crank another click, then another, on the jib. RD brought the traveler up as the boat came to speed, fine-tuning the mainsail. It felt good, doing something. It beat sitting in the cockpit waiting for the next drenching.

"Jib's got a rip!" It was Joe Dugan with the bad news.

"Where?" RD.

"Halfway up the leech."

"How bad?"

"Just started. Maybe four inches. Leech line's holding it together."

RD stuck his head below. "Get 3A ready."

Sargent: "Take your time. Get number three down, go bareheaded. We'll get 3A ready."

Dugan moved toward the mast, got ready to lower the jib halyard. Andy worked his way to the foredeck with RD behind him. It was tough going. The drill was to hang on when the boat plunged, then move after the water receded. Caskie stood by to ease the jib sheet. On the leeward side, forward of the mast, Andy and RD were often in water up to their knees, heavy water, lots of it, moving fast, hitting them like fifty-pound bags of poultry feed. They stayed low, hung on. RD yelled at Dugan to start the halyard. Caskie Kolegeri eased the sheet, then joined Andy and RD because now the flailing jib was coming down and all it wanted to do was tear itself away and disappear into the night. Andy had made his way forward to get the jib luff started down its captive foil. Wet and flailing, the jib resisted, but it was coming down a foot at a time. RD, behind Andy, was gathering the sail and trying to keep it corralled, passing the soaked, stiff fabric back to Kolegeri.

The boat dove into a particularly steep wave. The bow went under, scooping up green water that lifted Andy off the deck. He smacked into RD, and was halfway overboard when he got to Caskie, who grabbed him around the neck like he'd tackle a runner in the open field, dragged him over the lifelines to the deck, and hung on until the water drained away.

"Where you goin'?" Caskie asked.

Caskie spotted the clip of Andy's safety harness lying on his chest. He picked it up.

"You weren't clipped on?"

Andy was stunned. He had clipped on. He quickly got off the deck, went back to collecting the sail that was half overboard by now. On the way by he checked to see that RD was okay. He'd given him a good bump. RD nodded. Andy clipped on and got back to work.

It took the three men a full ten minutes to get the number three back on board and disconnected. Constantly pelted by green water, they wrestled the wet mess aft, leaving it in the cockpit under foot until the new sail got fed up from below. Wrestling the turtle out of the hatch and dragging it forward was brutal work. It was quickly soaking wet, heavy as lead. It was another ten minutes on the foredeck getting the #3A out of the turtle and into the feeder clip that led it into the foil, halyard clipped on, sheets tied on. Progress was interrupted by the boat pitching and slamming. The extra weight on the foredeck didn't help. And sailing without the jib slowed them down, gave the seas more control. Finally, Duncan started the halyard that was led to the vacant weather jib winch where Caskie cranked. His brother Larry had come on deck when the 3A was passed up, and handled the jib winch while Andy came back aft and trimmed.

"Great job, guys," Stuart yelled over the racket. "We've got speed. Always loved that 3A. I often sleep with it."

"Your kind of girl, Stu" came from Larry's direction.

The new tack put the boat on a friendlier angle through the seas that Andy estimated were in the ten-foot range. It seemed the wind had dropped a couple knots, and the instruments agreed. Spray still stung the face, but it wasn't quite as heavy. Big hits were less frequent.

Andy did his second hour at the wheel; then RD, the watch captain, sent him and Dugan below. "Stu, Caskie, and I have got this," RD said. "Get some rest." Andy didn't argue. Neither did Joe Dugan.

Crouse was still in the bunk they shared, so Andy crashed on a turtle, very glad to be out of the elements. He kept his gear on. He was wet inside, but somehow not soaked. The wet was contained by the latest synthetic fabrics he was wearing, meaning it was on the warm side. He closed his eyes and quickly went into alpha sleep, a nice trick he had learned at an astronomy conference. Astronomers are night owls who know how to sustain themselves during those long, dark periods tracking various objects. Andy had learned that twenty minutes in alpha was worth several hours of deep sleep, and it didn't knock you out. It was how fighter pilots got through the war. Ten minutes to takeoff? Alpha, here I come. It was more meditation than sleep, and it cleared the mind. Awareness of the situation remained. Thoughts, memories, and fantasies came and went.

Memories, like him clipping on as he went forward to douse the jib. His safety harness was a Lirakis, made by a guy he'd met. It had a twelve-foot scope of webbing with two strong clips sewn in. Good goods. As you moved, before you unclipped one, you clipped on the other. On the foredeck a clip-on line running fore and aft had been rigged to allow for more freedom of movement. That had been Andy's last clip-on. He ran the mental video, saw the high-visibility, half-inch yellow polypropylene line, pictured it lying on the deck, felt its slightly prickly surface, could hear the snap of the clip as he had engaged it. No question he had clipped on. Or had he missed the line as the boat lurched? Or had the clip failed? Still in alpha, eyes closed, one hand moved to his belt, felt the clip. It was intact. What could that mean? Not now. Let it go. Fatigue winning, alpha coming on like warm gravy. Becky kissing him, feet tingling. Smiling. Necking with Becky in the sail loft, just kids, so hot. The two of them sailing. Deedee hitting that backhand. Bam! The gunshot, the boat slamming into a good one, the bicycle down, Mitch swinging at him, seeing stars, drifting in space, foot dripping blood, off on his alpha adventure.

XIV

NEPTUNE

"It sounds impossible, I agree, but the guy still has more patients than he can handle. He had to take on a partner!" Joe Dugan was talking from the wheel.

Dawn was breaking. It was quite spectacular, one of those cloudless, clear mornings with unlimited visibility, the ocean calm as a lake, wind under five knots moving *All American* through the glassy water with just a ripple of a wake. Not good for racing, but one of those special mornings Andy would never forget. The peace, the isolated calm of such a morning as *All American* approached the equator, a thousand miles from land, the crew suspended in a tiny craft roughly two miles above the ocean floor, was ethereal. RD's watch was silent, as the birth of a new day bathed everything in harsh yellow light. Dimaris and Sargent slipped up from below to catch the moment.

The wind had crapped out an hour before the Davis watch had taken over at two a.m. With the proper, lightest heads'l up, there wasn't a whole lot to do but watch the sails and put some weight to leeward. RD had given the helm to Joe Dugan.

It was a happy group that morning. Frustration over the wind state had been dismissed by Sargent, reminding his crew that it was quite pointless to waste energy over what they could not control. Teddy Bosworth, on Sargent's watch, had been particularly freaked out by the onset of the calm conditions. Bosworth had taken to complaining about it every five minutes or so, driving himself and everyone else crazy. "Teddy," Sargent had finally said to him, quietly, "Shut up. Save your energy, man, because you're gonna need it. Stay calm so you'll feel the conditions changing and be ready to react to them. That's racing, what we're out here for, not ranting, which is a distraction."

The next watch was happy because driving was an activity that always caused Dugan to talk his head off. Nobody minded because Joe was always entertaining. He spoke very quietly, as if he were talking to himself. Feedback wasn't necessary. He was driving, paying attention, keeping his head focused on the sails, the wind instruments, the speed; and talking. Joe didn't seem to care if anyone was listening. Although feedback made his conversation more interesting.

Joe didn't disappoint. His brother was on his mind. No one knew Joe had a brother. That seemed to focus attention. Family stuff was always a juicy subject, and it was all safe there in outer space under the cover of darkness, in the secure vault of a race boat. Safer than Fort Knox.

It turned out Joe's brother was a veterinarian. Seemed he'd had a passion for animals as a kid that had stayed with him as he got older. He had always wanted to be a vet, so he'd studied hard and had been accepted by the University of Pennsylvania's well-known vet school. He'd graduated with honors, hung out a shingle. Then the problem started.

"He found himself not paying much attention to the animals he didn't like," Joe Dugan had said. "Giving them short shrift."

"Amazing," RD said.

"Hey, I can understand that. It makes sense," said Stu Samuels. "But one question: that problem had never come up before?"

"No. I asked him that," Joe said. "The pets we had at home we all liked, or my father would move them on if they were troublesome, you know, bad actors. Once my dad caught one of our cats, Alan, pissing on the marble tabletop in the kitchen. He'd been trying for weeks to discover which of our three cats was leaving the smelly dried-up puddle on the table. We had a family meeting about it. Dad was good with animals. That's probably where Paul got it from. Dad explained that while Alan was a fine cat, there was something about our environment that gave him a problem. Alan expressed it by pissing on the table. We were sad, but we got it. Paul and I were charged with finding Alan a new home. And we did. It all worked out."

"Who took him?" Stu Samuels asked. "Alan. Ha. Great name for a cat."

"Dad named him after Alan Ladd, the actor. Actually an older lady a couple streets over took him. We got to visit him."

"He never pissed on her table?" Stu asked.

"No. I don't think so." That got a laugh.

"At vet school I guess they had a variety of animals they practiced on and observed, whatever," Dugan continued. "They were people's pets, but Paul and his pals were studying, so it didn't matter much I guess."

"He hangs out a shingle," Caskie asked, "and some woman brings in a little puffball that won't stop barking, and it bites him and he says 'take this freaking spoiled little shit of a dog out of here'?"

Joe laughed. "Paul wouldn't have done that. Too polite. But he told me several of his patients were bugging him. He found himself ignoring them. For one reason or another, he just didn't like them." Dugan paused. "Roger, whaddathink about the halyard tension on the heads'l . . . maybe a little ease?"

Davis got up, walked slowly and carefully forward up the leeward side so as not to disturb what momentum the boat had. He played the flashlight over the sail, then walked back. "I think it's good."

"Pets are like people," Dugan said, picking up where he left off. "Good ones, bad ones, some you like, some you don't. Ask me how I know. I'm a P.A. A vet's patients can't say what's wrong with them. Vets really get into studying animal behavior so they can look for clues about what might be ailing them. Some vets, like Paul, go the extra mile, dig into animal personality. Paul said to me one time that animals are like any other group — and by that he meant groups like teachers, musicians, builders, lawyers — in that there are some really fine people at the top, some seriously mean-ass losers at the bottom, and the rest are in the middle somewhere. The old bell curve works for animals."

Joe went quiet for a moment, focusing on the instruments as a little six-knot gust dusted the boat. Andy, who was watching the jib, trimmed a click with the pressure, then eased as the puff moved on. Listening to Joe made Andy wonder how his dogs were. They were staying with Jeff while he was away. They liked Jeff.

"Paul tried different things," Joe continued as he responded to a ten-degree wind shift to the right. "Down ten." RD entered the time in a little notebook he kept in his shirt pocket. "First he would tell the owner of a dog he didn't like that another vet was better at treating the dog's particular illness. But he realized he couldn't use that all the time. Then he thought he'd say he didn't have room for another patient, but that was a crock since he'd just started his practice." Joe paused. "Back up ten degrees." Davis made a note.

"Wha'd'e do?" Stu Samuels asked.

"He decided to come right out with it," Joe said. "That's like Paul. He hates bullshit. Takes after my dad. He just went for it. He got his receptionist to tell first-time callers that their initial appointment would be like an interview, free, no charge, unless he decided to take the case and begin treatment."

"You mean he might refuse the case, tell the owner and his sick puppy to bag ass?" Stu said.

"That's about the size of it," Joe said.

"People didn't freak out?"

"No, because Paul is a very cool guy, and he developed a great rap about the critical importance of a vet being able to relate to an animal. He never told anyone he didn't like their animal, just that he was having a hard time relating to the animal, and if he couldn't relate to it, it was going to be very difficult for him to treat it."

"That's freakin' brilliant," Caskie said.

"It also makes sense," Joe said, "and also, Paul really believes it."

"Caskie, could you please sit on the low side?"

Caskie moved.

"I'm betting owners were very involved in this process," Stu said with a chuckle.

"Yeah, that's really the brilliant part," Joe said. "Some of the time it was the pet's owner who was the bad actor Paul didn't want to have to deal with."

"This is so cool," Caskie said. "And it worked out? He's still in business?"

"Thriving," Joe said. "He changed the name of his practice to Vet Pet Connect. He lives in a small town. Word got around, and it became a thing if you and your pet got to be one of Paul's patients. If you passed muster, if you were accepted. A feather in your cap, a member of an exclusive club. There was no list of those who were turned away, but the gossip was intense. Hey," Joe whispered, "did you hear Mrs. Jones and Fifi weren't accepted?"

"Mrs. Jones and Fifi." Stuart cracked up. "Can you imagine, Mrs. Jones who tries to run everything in town in that snotty way of hers, always with that rotten little fluffer tagging along with its sparkly collar and the little red bow in its hair . . . Mrs. Jones being rejected! Mrs. Jones! Ha ha ha, what a hoot. I'm gonna get a dog and move to wherever Paul lives so Buster and I can be his patient."

"You'd never be accepted," Caskie said.

"He should make it a franchise," Stu said. "Vet Pet Connect. I love it."

"Wish I could do it with my patients," Joe said.

All American crossed the equator at high noon. Barely. They were hardly moving. The mains'l hung slack. The jib had been lowered. But it was a special moment for Larry and Caskie Kolegeri, and for Andy. None of them had ever crossed the equator before, meaning they would be subject to a certain amount of harassment, a dubious seafaring tradition with mysterious origins. Over the years, those with enthusiasm for carrying out elaborate and distressing harassment in the name of initiation had taken the rigors of the initial crossing of the equator to brutal lengths that included beatings, sexual assaults, even a few deaths. The U.S. Navy was forced to write regulations to temper the potentially harmful, equator-crossing hazing rituals.

Race boats were not exempt from the tradition, although one might think that life aboard those stripped-down vessels where life's necessities, not to mention comfort, were reduced to conditions the Humane Society would condemn was punishment enough. A priority of every man aboard every boat in the race was keeping his personal gear as dry and as organized as possible. Having one's stuff interfered with was a nightmare. Andy had heard tales about what other first-timers had endured, including having motor oil poured in their boots; having their clothing soaked in saltwater and tied in knots;

themselves being stripped and given a full-body shave. Andy had considered lying about having made a previous crossing. But he knew he would be found out, and decided to just let it happen.

That was why at high noon, in board-shrinking, 105-degree heat, under a blue, cloudless sky, Andy found himself sitting in the cockpit alongside the Kolegeri brothers, naked except for the speedo bathing suit he wore as skivvies, and pouring sweat.

Jan Sargent came up the companionway as King Neptune, complete with a long white beard he'd purchased for the occasion, using a towel as a robe, with a makeshift trident made from a boat hook. Sargent was the right man for the part. In an instant, he had become Neptune. RD and Richard Crouse were his lackeys. Davis held a large pot from the galley with the handle of a ladle protruding from it.

Sargent had his best Lord of the Deep voice on as he read from a document about equatorial traditions. "Sailors undergoing one ceremony," Sargent read, "were physically and verbally abused before having a dark liquid daubed over their naked bodies, then forced to jump overboard until allowed back on the vessel."

Sargent paused and looked up, his face fierce as he addressed the three men seated before him. "And so, you dirty tadpoles, you come before me because you have sinned. And what is your sin, tadpole Caskie?"

"I released the jib when we tacked, your elegance."

"A vile sin if there ever was one. Christen our friend with the stew of Neptune!"

Davis advanced on Caskie, scooped up a brimming ladle of a frothy, slimy mix of coffee grounds, chunks of meat that had gone bad and been saved for this moment, moldy hunks of bread, very old banana slices, dish soap, and with a cup or two of old motor oil added for thickening.

"Absolve this dirty tadpole of his sins," Neptune pronounced as RD dumped several ladles of stew over Caskie's head and shoulders, making sure it ran down across his face.

Larry received similar treatment after admitting he had brushed his teeth every time he went on watch. Then came Andy.

"And dirty tadpole Andy, you look like a very bad sinner to me. Confess!"

"I am the boss's son," Andy muttered, already revolted by the bad smell of the stew that had splashed on him when Davis had dumped it on Larry.

"The boss's son!" Neptune roared, and laughed maniacally as the rest of the crew howled and applauded. "The boss's son . . . tell me, could there be a worse sin?"

"Nooooo," the crew intoned as one.

"His redemption will require the max," Neptune railed. "You know what to do," he said to Davis.

Davis emptied the pot on Andy's head, shaking out the residue stuck to the bottom, the chunks of vile stuff, the coffee grounds, until Andy was covered in the gross mix. David left the pot on Andy's head.

"Boil boil, trouble and toil," Neptune muttered. "Ah, if we'd only had an eye of newt! But we are almost done here with our miracle of converting hopeless dirty tadpoles into strong salts of the sea. But first they must sit here in the hot, equatorial sun for a few minutes and let this stew, this stew of salvation, bake into their very pores."

The three sat immobile, heads down, dirty tadpoles, unhappy tadpoles to say the very least. The pot slipped off Andy's head and fell with a clang into the cockpit. The crew made derisive comments.

Pete Dimaris had popped below, having heard an electronic sound that indicated an incoming fax. Now he came back up the companionway, a sheet of paper in hand. "It's for you," Dimaris said, extending the sheet to Andy.

Andy looked up, wiped a hand across his eyes, then took the sheet. He stared at it for a long minute, his face expressionless beneath its layer of stew. He let the sheet drop onto the wet mess of the cockpit floor. Then he slowly stood up. "Son of a bitch!" he screamed into the empty void of sky, sea, and horizon, startling the crew into silence. "Son of a bitch," Andy repeated, quietly. Then he dove over the side.

Sargent turned to Dimaris. "What did it say?" Dimaris shrugged.

Joe Dugan had gingerly picked up the stew-soaked sheet and was looking at it. "Not much," he said. "Slightly difficult to read: 'Mountain View . . . has hit the wall.'"

"All right. Fish that newly christened strong salt out of the water," Sargent said, pulling off his beard, "and the three of you clean up this mess you've made."

XV

PORT

"Lights!"

It was Dave Zimmer's voice, loud and clear, exulting over the glow he'd identified dead ahead indicating that land in the shape of Punta del Este, Uruguay, was not far off. Land, after twenty days. Not a long time compared to the endless early voyages in the old square-riggers, but it was relative. In today's world, how many people other than a handful of yachtsmen, a few astronauts, scientists on research vessels, or sailors on extended military missions could say they had been away from dry land for twenty days? Or even one day. After twenty days, body rhythm changed along with one's priorities. Eating and sleeping habits had changed, as had one's social life, and normal communication — the daily intake of news, gossip, music, and the endless bombardment of earthly noise — had been eliminated. After twenty days, *All American*'s crew didn't know whether to dread land, or embrace it.

"Fried chicken," Jan Sargent said. That, everyone could agree on.

Zimmer's clarion call woke Andy, whose dream had him on his mountain bike again, taking big air as he landed in a gravel patch and skidded into a damp tunnel where his blood-drenched father, looking like the walking dead, was coming for him, his face a frightening mask of rage, screaming "Bastard!" over and over. It had been nearly eight days since they'd been becalmed crossing the equator. The wind had returned with a vengeance, and *Double-A*, as the boat had come to be known among the crew, had eaten up the miles like an athletic thoroughbred on a heavy dose of performance-enhancing drugs. It had been a wild ride, wet, noisy, uncomfortable, and frightening, four things Jan Sargent considered the essence of winning. "Show me a dry, comfortable crew," he had said during one particularly crazy night, "and I'll show you a bunch of losers." Sargent knew how to stimulate his team.

Most of the eight days had been spent humoring *Double-A*. Like some crazed honey badger, the boat had impossible behavior in mind that could only spell self-destruction if not curtailed. The wind, which had averaged over thirty knots much of the time, had been mostly on the beam, any monohull's fastest point of sailing. But with a light flier like *All American*, that was also the most perilous point of sail because it meant managing sail combinations that wouldn't overpower the boat but would still be sufficient to allow the helmsman to maintain control. Not enough sail, and the seas would have their way with the boat. But if the boat were overpowered, if it were to break loose and round up, the boom would be dragging in the water and the pressure of such a knockdown could tear the mainsail apart, or break the mast. That would be fun. A thousand miles from nowhere with no mast, and possible serious injuries.

The sea had also been up, and the boat was sailing beam-on, requiring the helmsmen to find a friendly path through the steep troughs — tearing down the back of one wave, driving up the front of the next — without getting smacked by the wave tops that were usually breaking. The combination of wind speed and angle had perished any thought of carrying the spinnaker.

Such conditions had a way of wiping out all earthly drama, no matter how crucial it might have previously seemed. The tumultuous world of agitated ocean, and an unbroken dome of sky, were all that existed. Life on an unstable platform, subject to nature's whims, with the barest of cover provided by this fragile vessel of fiberglass, became totally consuming. Andy could imagine how astronauts must feel, how becoming weightless must quickly reduce land to a faded memory.

The work on deck was back-breaking. Just hanging on, dealing with the boat's abrupt, radical motion, was a constant challenge. The watches retired exhausted, with crewmen quickly falling out in their gear on bunks and sail turtles. Two or three hours before Zimmer's call, the wind had mercifully abated and come slightly ahead. The reef was shaken out of the main, and a larger heads'l was raised. When Andy awoke, *All American* had the rail down and was making twelve knots sailing on a close reach in fifteen knots of wind. By comparison, the boat felt steady, comfortable. Andy had to laugh. By comparison.

Still blitzed by his dream, he realized with some amazement he hadn't thought about Mountain View for several days. Jeff Linn's cryptic fax came back to him like a sledgehammer. The immensity of losing Mountain View, and the generous hunk of his personal fortune that he had put into it, made him glad he was still lying down. Such a colossal failure was too much to contemplate. Nothing to be done until he could talk with Linn. There he was, ocean and sky, nothing to be accomplished on the unreliable satellite phone. He recalled Jan Sargent getting after Teddy Bosworth for ranting about being becalmed when crossing the equator. "Don't waste energy over what you can't control," Sargent had told Bosworth. Beyond the bluster, and his standup act designed for public consumption, Sargent was a smart dude.

Eric Menici was up, as usual, bent over his editing machine looking at clips his onboard cameras had filmed during the heavy weather. Andy peered over Eric's shoulder at the images he'd captured of spray flying and large seas coming aboard.

"Man. Glad I wasn't on that boat."

"Me too."

"I know it's frowned upon, but since we're close, can I get a message to a guy I need to speak with, let him know I'll be available soon?"

"Yep. Gimme his phone."

"Here it is. Thanks. I owe you one."

"A plate of fried chicken." Eric chuckled.

Andy handed Jeff's card to Eric with this note scribbled on the back: "Punta close. Talk in four hours."

"Got it, 10-4 and all that. You'll be an hour ahead in Punta, don't forget."

As dawn broke, *All American* crossed the finish line, one end of which was the 140-foot Faro de Punta del Este, the lighthouse that had been blinking at them every eight seconds for the past two hours. Engine on, sails down, flaked and turtled, and everyone on deck as they were welcomed by thirty or so hearty souls who had taken their boats out to greet them. As they rounded the long pier of the Marinas del Puerto, everyone drew a quick breath of disappointment as they saw *Ram Bunctious* parked in the slip reserved for first-to-finish.

"Goddamn calm at the equator," Terry Bosworth muttered. Later they would learn that the Kiwi boat had beaten them in by twenty-nine minutes. Not bad after 6,000 miles.

They'd barely gotten their dock lines secure when a delivery guy appeared with a huge box of fried chicken and a case of beer. Sargent's work. The crew dove in as if they hadn't eaten in a month. The local TV channel filmed the feeding frenzy, then climbed on board. Jan Sargent suddenly appeared in a clean shirt and team jacket, looking salty but very cool, and gave the local station's crew everything they could have hoped for.

"Were you surprised to see *Ram Bunctious* when you turned the corner?" the presenter asked.

"No, not at all," Sargent said. "Those boys are good. We have our work cut out. And by the way, can you suggest a good liquor store? I have a bet to pay off."

Well-briefed, the presenter grabbed the boss's son. Andy didn't realize how exhausted he was until he found himself under the lights staring into the glass eye of the camera. The confusion of land was instantly upon him. Right then he understood why the Arctic tern transfers to an outgoing vessel when the vessel it's hitched a ride on gets close to land. Andy had fought with all he had to avoid going on this race. He'd been wet and varying degrees of uncomfortable for three weeks. Now with the presenter shoving a microphone in his face, he realized he was already missing the peace, the tranquility, even the crazy high-speed sailing of open ocean. Water and sky. He found himself mumbling something about the first American boat in the race, the proud sponsorship of Moss Optics, and what a great boat *All American* was before the boys came to his rescue with cheers and cold beers, interview over with a good closing shot.

Andy scanned the dock hoping he might see Becky, but it was Isha who was seen working her way through the crowd. Isha, who was looking very good after three weeks, wearing a revealing top of soft fabric over tights that left little to the imagination. "Dressing the curves," she liked to say. Stu Samuels was standing beside Andy, watching Isha's approach with obvious delight. "Fried chicken might come in second, eh?" Stu said, nudging Andy, who cracked up. Then he thought about the phone call.

Isha had a limo waiting, of course. On the way to the Iberia Hotel, Andy put his arm around her. She pulled away. "God, you smell horrible," she said, and that ended that. The hotel wasn't far. They both got out. The driver pulled Andy's fragrant bag of damp gear out of the trunk.

"Here's the key," Isha said. "I have errands. See you in a while. Take a shower, take two showers, please!"

"My phone. Did you get me a phone?"

Isha dug in her bag. "Yes, but it's quite worthless." She handed it to Andy, and hustled off.

In the room he dropped his bag and made a call to Jeff on the house phone. Busy. Really? At seven a.m.? "Call me."

He dug in his bag and pulled out his powerful little Stealth Scope, a prototype for a high-end upgrade Moss was considering, and walked to the window. The fifth floor gave him a good angle over the trees in the park adjacent to the hotel. He could see faces clearly many blocks away. Amazing. He put it down, dialed Jeff again. Busy. "Call me, damn it."

Andy picked up the scope, returned to the window, and browsed. Whoa, wait a minute, damned if it wasn't Isha, stepping out, what a walk, shaking it, ought to be illegal, on a mission, looking at her watch. What is she up to, sitting on a bench at a bus stop? She's definitely not waiting for a bus. Isha taking a bus? Funny idea. Isha looking around. Wait, she's meeting someone, a guy. Heavyset, black ponytail, wearing jeans and a sweat-stained shirt, untucked. Andy watched as the two of them had a conversation. What the hell . . . ? Isha got up, crossed the street, and walked into the Scotiabank. The guy remained on the bench.

The phone rang. Man, he was tired, could hardly think. Two fast beers on the boat hadn't helped. He was hungry. He'd gotten one piece of chicken before the TV reporter had grabbed him. Now he was watching Isha meeting some guy on the streets of Punta del Este. Andy had stepped off the boat less than an hour ago and he was already feeling beat-up. Bloody hell. Fucking land!

Jeff Linn wasn't much help. He didn't know much. Neither George Cooper, whom Andy had hired to organize the Mountain View Corporation when Mitch had rejected the idea as a project for Moss, nor Cooper's secretary could be reached. Oh, yeah, Andy had taken the astronomy-resort idea to Mitch, thinking for one terribly misguided moment that it would improve his otherwise dismal reputation in the company. In his most haughty, dismissive manner, Mitch had said no thanks, that Moss's business was to make optical products, not start "theme parks." When George Cooper had come along, Andy had been delighted. With a degree in planetary science, plus being a savvy businessman, George was perfect for the job. Now, after two years, he was gone? How . . . ? Jeff said he'd been trying to find him for ten days. Checks were due. Creditors were calling.

"You can write checks," Andy reminded Jeff.

There was a pause.

"What?!" Andy barked, impatient.

"The account has been locked," Jeff said quietly.

Andy had flopped on the bed and was staring at a small crack in the ceiling. "Are you kidding? Have you talked with the bank? Are you serious? Okay, look, I just got off the freaking boat. I need food. I need sleep. I need to get laid. I need to jump out the goddamn window. Speaking of getting laid, not. With that neat little scope you designed I just saw Isha on the street having a meeting with some funky dude. We'll talk later. Okay?"

"Some funky dude?"

"Yeah."

"Maybe one of the crew?"

"No, man. Some street dude. Look, Jeff, I don't know, don't ask me. Maybe I imagined it. Maybe I imagined I just did twenty days on the open ocean in a dinghy. Maybe I'm actually dead. I know I'm toast. We need to think this out. See what you can learn. Make some calls. Call Sam Cotton. He's been there forever. He and Deedee are close. Tell him you're calling for me. Tell him everything. He can be trusted. Okay?" Andy stared at the crack in the ceiling looking for answers, or maybe bugs. "Wait. One thing. I'm trying to remember how we met George Cooper, how he came into our lives."

There was a pause. "That was two years ago," Jeff said. "Not sure. I think I heard about him through you. Wasn't he a friend of Isha's?"

"Yeah," Andy said, his head slowly spinning. "I think that's right."

Andy managed to get the phone into the receiver before he fell asleep. Eight hours later he woke up and again was staring at the crack in the ceiling. Had it gotten bigger? He wondered what the bad smell was, and realized it was him. He was starved. He called room service and ordered steak and eggs, then went into the bathroom. He caught sight of himself in the mirror and was shocked at the gaunt, rugged face staring back at him; the tousled hair unwashed for three weeks, the growth of beard and moustache, the red eyes, the cracked lips. It was a face he hadn't seen in weeks, a face he hadn't ever seen. He pulled off his shirt and saw muscles he didn't recognize. His arms were defined. His stomach was flat, his pecs showing. And the bruises, must be half a dozen good abrasions and black-and-blue marks on arms and chest he didn't remember getting. There was some old dried blood. His hands were a sight, scarred and calloused, cracked and salted.

Isha's array of cosmetics took up most of the sink shelf. He grabbed her electric toothbrush and went at it, then jumped in the shower. He was out by the time the food arrived.

The phone woke Andy. He'd slept another few hours. It was Isha. "Sorry I didn't get back but I ran into Roger Davis's girlfriend Gloria who is here and she and Roger have rented this little apartment with a great view of the water so I've been hanging out with her because I know how much you needed to sleep so I thought I wouldn't bother you, wasn't that nice of me?"

Andy recognized an Isha monologue in full flight, so he said nothing.

"Anyway, listen, we have this cool plan for later, a great spot, very local, very get-down Punta if you know what I mean, good drinks, great local food, great guitar player I hear. The limo will pick you up at eight out front. I'll go with Gloria and Roger because it's very close to where they are."

"Don't you need to change?"

"No no, this is dress-down, very, you'll see. I'll be fine. I bought this very Punta blouse that shows Them off very nicely I think you'll agree."

"I'm actually more eager to get down with you and Them than hit one of Punta's low spots, if you know what I mean." Andy was firing for effect.

"Oh baby, I know, but later we'll have the whole rest of the night to play, okay?"

Andy smiled. "Sounds good to me." He was hearing a disturbingly evident undertone in everything Isha said. It had a name: bullshit.

Three hours later Andy was sitting at the bar at Señor Rico's, a run-down joint in a rough section of the city. Although he had to admit the *chivito* steak sandwich had been damn good. And the guitar player had some chops. But now he was pretty drunk, enjoying the company of several local guys who were amused by this American sailor who was buying them drinks and pouring out his heart to them. They had learned about this girl Becky who he fancied, how he'd known her since they were kids, and another girl, Isha, who was looking like trouble, she'd actually always been trouble, and some bad business deal, something to do with a mountain that was falling apart. Crazy American guy. He kept asking if this Isha woman had called, if there was a message. "She's two hours late, man, and that's a lot even for Isha." That brought laughter from Andy's new friends, who were making jokes about him in Spanish, and repeating a few English, all-purpose clichés.

Around eleven o'clock Andy decided to give it up. The evening had gone south like everything else. Had he been in the wrong place? Naw, the limo driver would have known. Isha had given him the address. But it sure wasn't her kind of place, this Señor Rico's. Had something happened to Roger and Gloria? Or Isha? He'd better get back to the hotel, call it a night. He paid his tab, exposing a large bill as he left a generous tip, then shook hands all around as he pulled himself together and left.

Andy had barely gotten to the sidewalk when he realized he had company. He recognized two of the guys from a table in the back of the bar. There was a third, rough-looking, with flat eyes. Before Andy could get his bearings, the third guy had given him a shove that knocked him to the ground. Andy fished in his pocket, pulled out the ten-thousand-peso note, and held it out.

"Okay," he said.

The rough guy laughed, quietly pulled a knife, and snapped out the blade with a flick of his wrist. The sound raised the hairs on Andy's neck. Andy looked at each of the men. For a moment he was totally cowed, intimidated, his back against the wall, outnumbered by serious-looking, badass toughs. Old Andy. He reverted to money. "More tomorrow," he said. "I get more tomorrow."

"Bastid!" Knife Man spit it out like a wad of tobacco juice.

The word went through Andy like an electric charge, triggering a reaction he'd never felt before. Then he registered the man's black ponytail, the sweat-stained, untucked shirt. A surge of adrenaline overcame the alcohol. He got to his feet slowly, and extended the bill to Knife Man, who reached for it with his left hand as he readied the knife to strike. Andy's sudden attack caught him off guard. The knife sliced along Andy's forearm as he struck Knife Man in the throat, hard, with his fist. The weapon fell to the sidewalk. Knife Man began choking, gasping for air. Andy was on him like a mad dog, landing blow after blow. The others tried to jump in, but blind rage combined with the hardened shape he was in made them no match for Andy. He flung them away like it was some choreographed movie fight. Hurting, they ran off, leaving Andy to pound Knife Man into unconsciousness.

Andy heard people running toward him. He rolled off Knife Man and sprang to his feet, looking for the weapon. "Whoa, take it easy." It was Jan Sargent and Eric Menici. Andy's knees suddenly felt weak. Jan and Eric grabbed him, held him up until he caught his breath.

"You're bleeding like a stuck pig," Sargent said, pulling a bandana from his back pocket and wrapping Andy's arm. "What's this?" Sargent gently pulled the bloodied ten-thousand-peso note from Andy's still-clenched fist.

"He wouldn't make change."

"What brought you to this lovely part of town?"

"A limo," Andy said, still out of breath. "I might ask you the same thing."

The three of them laughed. Eric squatted down, checked Knife Man. "Sleeping soundly. He'll live."

"That's very good news," Sargent said. "You take on the whole bar?"

"Three, I think," Andy said. "Felt like the whole bar."

"You okay?"

"You know," Andy said, "I feel pretty good. Pretty damn good."

"Let's blow this joint, unless you plan to invite the police to have a drink," Sargent said. As he was getting up, Eric saw a crumpled envelope next to Knife Man's form. "Scotiabank" was printed on it. He quietly picked up the envelope and stuck it in his jeans.

XVI

BUSINESS

Given the amount of blood on Andy's clothes, the late hour, and their altered states, Andy, Jan, and Eric entered the Iberia Hotel by the back entrance and took the service elevator to the fifth floor. They encountered no one. In the room Andy rushed to the toilet, long overdue. He noticed Isha's cosmetic array was gone, neatly packed in a bag perched on the vanity.

He unlocked the fridge and the three of them grabbed mini bottles of tequila and beers for a nightcap. Andy turned on the TV. *Teenage Mutant Ninja Turtles* appeared. Eric went to the bathroom, soaked a hand towel in hot water, removed the bandana, and washed the cut on Andy's arm. "Not bad," Eric said, as the hot compress made Andy wince. "In my hood, anything under six inches was considered a scratch."

The three of them stared in amusement at *Ninja Turtles*, which somehow made more sense in Spanish, content to sit and unwind. Then Sargent popped the question.

"What was that all about?"

"Guess they figured I was an easy mark," Andy said.

"But Señor Rico's? Come on, man, that's really off the beaten path."

"Mistake I guess. Maybe the limo driver was in on it. Dunno." Andy shrugged. "Good sandwich."

"And a guy with a knife?" Sargent persisted. "Three guys couldn't relieve a half-drunk American sailor of a few pesos? They needed a knife?"

"Turns out they did!" Andy said with a grin.

The three of them howled at that just as Isha arrived. All she could see from the door was Jan and Eric. From her perspective, Andy was out of sight. Isha walked into her room at midnight to find a couple guys from All America's crew whom she hardly knew drinking and watching television, laughing, and obviously quite drunk — in her room goddammit! — and she started to go off until she took a couple steps and saw Andy, a vision that stopped her in her tracks and performed the formidable task of shutting her up, instantly. It was momentary, Isha was that good, but the split second of her face being re-arranged into a mask of disbelief was what Andy would retain as palpably as if it were a photo he carried in his wallet.

"Oh my God, look at you, the blood . . . You never showed up!" Isha said, quickly going on the offense as she regained her momentum. Jan and Eric sat back and marveled at one of Isha's more prolonged and inventive monologues. Andy got in a line or two about being taken to Señor Rico's where he'd had a few drinks and waited for three hours, then had to fight off muggers. Isha took it from there. Eric was so entranced by this demonstration of Isha's ability to talk ears off owls that he located the TV remote and reduced the volume of *Ninja Turtles*, a little at a time, the better to hear this very emotive woman, whose extreme choreographed moves as she spoke threatened to fling off the scanty clothing concealing her abundant charms at any second, carry on about what the plan had been and about Roger Davis and Gloria and the limo driver and how she'd told the bloody fool specifically to take Andy to Señor Roberto's, not Señor Rico's, my God, wherever in hell that is, and how they all had waited and waited for Andy to show up, and how they had tried to call him so many times and hadn't she said his phone was worthless here in South freaking America? And how they were worried about him and almost called the police and now she finds him here covered with blood and for God's sake (angrily addressing Jan and Eric directly), "why didn't you people take him to the hospital because isn't it obvious he needs medical attention?!"

It was all Jan and Eric could do not to applaud. "You people" resonated. It was a fantastic performance. But credit the two of them for being able to maintain blank faces, for seeming to take Isha's world seriously; for not wanting to queer whatever deal Andy had going. It was Andy who cracked up, Andy who found blessed relief at long last in what an outrageous piece of work he had on his hands, relief in his dawning appreciation of what a polished liar Isha was, and how her very act of lying was possibly unmatched for its entertainment value. As lying went, it was absolutely pornographic, and it cracked him up.

It had been difficult to confront the growing suspicion that Isha was a principle player in a nefarious plot to cause him serious harm. It was hard for him to get his head around that. He was working on it, but just a few minutes at a time because the concept was that remarkable, that outrageous. Helped, perhaps, by having spent twenty days at sea, the apparent Mountain View crisis, his presence in "South freaking America," the crazy events of the past evening, and how he, the useless, overweight, drunken rich kid had kicked the shit out of three toughs — one with a knife! — the whole thing cracked him up. Andy going off triggered Jan and Eric, blowing whatever control they had managed to employ, and now the three of them were howling. Eric had rolled out of his chair onto the floor, helpless.

That wasn't quite the reaction Isha had expected, and like any actress whose routine might have backfired, she was at once sad and angry. Seizing the moment, Andy was on his feet putting his arm around her. "Come on, honey," Andy said, encouraging Jan and Eric with a look over Isha's shoulder, "we're laughing with you, not at you. I mean, nobody can tell a story like you can." Jan and Eric nodded and murmured in agreement, and they didn't have to lie. Eric clapped.

"Really, you think so?" Isha was contrite, almost tearful as she tucked into Andy's arm.

"Absolutely." Andy's look at his teammates said wrap it up.

"I guess we'd better call it a night," Jan said, standing carefully, getting his bearings. Eric hauled himself off the floor with effort.

"I'm coming with you," Andy said. "Just let me get a bag."

"Oh baby no, stay here," Isha crooned, as her hand slipped down well below Andy's hip.

"Believe me, I'd love to," Andy said, having determined that his smart play for the moment was to apply bygones. "We've got an early meeting with race officials. Best if I'm waking up on-site and near a coffee pot."

"We have a coffee pot right here!"

"Yeah, and Eric did a good job on the nasty cut I got on the boat that opened up, but I need Joe Dugan to make sure it's not going to get infected."

"I'll be sad without you." Isha was pouting.

"Me too," Andy said. "Me too. But," he said, making eye contact, "business is business."

"I know," she said demurely, looking away.

The warm, clear night was full of music. It was a fancy affair, a fashion show laid on by the official hosts of the Punta stopover, with all proceeds going to charities. The crews of the eight competing yachts were seated at big tables in their team colors. Heavy hitters from all parts of the city had purchased tables. The men were in blazers and shirts open a button or perhaps two, depending on the quality of their physiques, the quantity of chest hair, and the carets of gold chains on display. The women were dressed to the nines, with display a given. A red carpet was set up, with TV crews providing live coverage. The venue was several acres of lush lawn mown to championship fairway standards flanked by an Olympic-size pool on one side and a grass tennis court on the other. On the back side was a full-size soccer goal, a reminder that the owner of this lavish estate was none other than internationally known footballer Colon Martinez, one of the wealthiest people in Uruguay. His sprawling designer mansion crowned a rise behind the stage and catwalk that had been built for the fashion show. Lou Sosa's rocking seventeen-piece tango band with maybe a thousand silver buttons flashing on the musicians' collective gaucho outfits made it all move.

Isha had outdone herself and was holding her own in the eye-candy department despite the impressive cream of local beauties, and the presence of stunning models who had been imported, and whose flashes of nudity could be glimpsed behind the transparent hedge where they were hastily changing. Isha had gone for a scanty arrangement of feather-light fabrics that seemed to move on their own in those rare moments when she was still. Her hair was in designer disarray, held precariously in check by a large, jeweled chignon pin. A shame, Andy thought as he watched her endless dance, that it was all such a shuck. He was surprised that the convoluted bit of violence that had been directed at him had stimulated more curiosity than fear. There was a game afoot. He was a player, and he felt suddenly quite alive and ready. He realized it was a new feeling, one he rather liked.

He and Jan were waiting backstage for their cue to join two models on the catwalk, someone's idea of an amusing thing to do, get the various teams involved in the show. There was no slipping out of it, and, as Jan had said, the company was good. Their lovely partners arrived, and the four of them walked the walk to the Sosa rhythms and the razzing from the other teams, lots of whistling and laughs, and then that was over as their models rushed off to change without so much as a nice-to-meet-you.

Back at the team table, Sam Cotton had arrived. Sam was looking dapper in blazer and tie. Andy couldn't get over how robust he looked. He'd lost some weight and his eyes had some sparkle. He was working on a glass of red as he chatted with the team. The minute Andy and Jan arrived he broke off conversation and got to his feet before they could sit down.

"We need to talk. I've arranged to go to the house."

Isha, missing nothing, swooped over, draping an arm around Sam Cotton's shoulder.

"Now where do you think you're going, you must stay . . ."

"Sorry, boat business." It was Jan, using his King Neptune voice, putting his arm around Cotton and claiming him with a laugh. It caught Isha off guard, and she turned away. Her pout was wasted on the skipper.

As Andy was leaving, Eric caught up with him.

"I thought you should have this," Eric said, handing him a small, soiled envelop, folded in half. "It's probably nothing, but I picked it up next to that guy you clobbered at the bar the other night. Forgot about it. Lucky I go through my pockets before I put my pants in the laundry. No idea if it's important. Thought you should have it. Just in case. Later."

Eric walked away. Andy unfolded the envelope

and saw "Scotiabank" printed on it. It stopped him for a second; then he recalled watching Isha with the Stealth Scope, watching her meet the same guy who'd pulled a knife on him that night, watching her walk into Scotiabank. He felt a chill. It made his arm hurt.

He caught up with Sam and Jan as they got to the house. The butler recognized Sam, and the three men followed his lead, making their way through several gorgeous rooms and hallways out of interior-design-magazine photographs to the library. There were books, sure enough, but the trophies and keepsakes, the signed photographs, balls, cleats, and jerseys outnumbered them. It was an impressive display. They were barely seated in soft, button-tufted leather chairs when a waitress appeared with a tray of drinks and warm nibbles.

The boat business took about ten minutes. Jan gave Sam a quick report on the leg, talking about tactics and how the yacht — and the crew — had behaved. A sailor, Sam understood. Jan told him no changes in personnel were necessary. It was a good team. Sam told Jan the two new sails had arrived, and gave him an envelope containing cash for local needs, and paperwork indicating bills paid.

"I'm not sure I understand this note you sent me indicating a 'leg bonus' of ten thousand dollars," Sam said. "Did you or one of the crew injure a leg?"

Jan smiled. "No sir. We finished in the top three, on the podium. The bonus is a race tradition."

"Ah," Sam said, returning the smile. "I'm afraid it is not a Moss tradition."

Jan shrugged. "No worries."

Andy loved it. There was Sam Cotton, old-school Sam who had recently turned eighty. Sam, whom he had known since childhood, short, stocky Sam looking fit, still with a good head of hair, albeit white, taking it to Jan Sargent. A couple of first-rate gamers having a go.

"I do have this little token for you," Sam said, pulling a thin, rectangular box from his jacket pocket. Jan took the gift, opened it, and extracted a Stealth Scope much like the one Andy had, only an older model. Andy could see Jan was touched. He got up, went to the window overlooking the stage, and put it to his eye.

"Wow." He looked back at Sam. "We're on the best side of that hedge."

Sargent walked back, but didn't sit. He picked up his papers, shook Sam's hand, gave Andy a wink, and left. Sam got up, followed him, and shut the door.

"You friend Jeff Linn called," Sam said, getting right to it.

"I know. I didn't intend for you to fly to South America," Andy said.

"Good excuse for a change of scenery. Besides, the course at the Cantegril Club is supposed to be excellent. Built in 1929. I have an eight-a.m. tee time tomorrow. Martinez set me up. Nice of him." Sam paused, poured himself more wine. Andy relished how calm he felt in Sam's presence. In this period of total suspension when not too much made any sense — the days at sea, the strange country, Isha's apparently threatening behavior, the fight that could have been very bad — having Sam there in the flesh was a reassuring connection to the familiar. Sam knew it. That was why he'd come.

"I'd bring you the hell home with me," Sam said, "but Deedee would have a bloody fit. She's adamant you finish the race. But Jesus, Andy . . . " Sam shook his head. "Jan told me about the fight. A knife? Are you kidding?"

"Yeah. Bad luck."

"Bullshit. There's been too many of these incidents. That business in the tunnel ten years ago, that could have been you. Jan told me about you damn near going over the side, not clipped on . . . "

"Damn, Sam, did you grill Jan?" Andy kept it light, but mention of the tunnel always struck his core. Sam lining it up with Knife Man gave it even more weight. Could it have been him? That had never occurred . . .

" . . . and I know that's bullshit because you've known to clip on since you were ten years old."

"I thought I had."

"You did! Who was on the foredeck working with you?"

"RD. Davis."

"Same guy who messed with you on the boulders at Outward Bound, right? Same guy who got a tray of food dumped in his lap."

"You got all this on video?" Andy laughed.

"I liked that, the food dump." Sam's grin was short-lived. "And now this Mountain Dew thing."

"View."

"It's getting to be a goddamn mountain all right. I don't like it."

"Have you found out anything?"

"Mitch spilled the details to Deedee," Sam said. "She was mad as hell when Mitch wouldn't let the company do

Mountain View. She found out, hell, Mitch probably told her, knowing she couldn't do anything about it but stew."

"What details, what did Mitch know? Sam, for chrissakes!"

"That George Cooper has vanished along with a lot of money. That's about all we know."

"People don't just vanish these days."

"Well, he has. Emptied the escrow account."

"Jesus. Are you kidding?! That needs both our signatures."

Sam just smiled. "This is a digital age, my boy. So things have ground to a halt, except for the lawsuits. But rest assured, Deedee is on your side. She told Mitch she would bail you out. You can imagine how that went down. He can't block it. I'm the trustee. So be nice to me."

Andy found himself staring at the ceiling again. No cracks this time. It was an extraordinary coffered ceiling, with a soccer ball carved into the center of each frame (Goal!), all done in dark Brazilian hardwoods.

"She's very proud of you for staying with the race, doing so well. Very proud."

Andy took a deep breath. "How's Becky? She didn't make it."

Sam gave Andy one of those looks that fathers cast upon young men who have the audacity to be interested in their daughters. It's somewhere between the look a potential buyer puts on a horse and the blank stare a detective lays on a suspect. "She's well," Sam said. "Busy. I heard she was thinking about coming here, but work interfered."

"I don't know what she does."

"Photographer with a law degree. Has a studio. Portraits, food, cars, you name it."

"Really!"

"Really." Both men laughed.

"I have to say you look really good, Sam, like you've turned the clock back."

"Thanks. I got sick of dragging my ass around, so I decided to do something about it. Changed my diet, started working out, playing more golf. I think it's the golf that really did it."

"I'm sure." Andy smiled.

Sam left around ten p.m. He and Andy had rejoined Jan and the team at the Moss table and had done justice to the delicious *asado* barbecue of beef, pork, chicken, and sausage that was served. Outside the gate a few taxis were lined up, their drivers sitting on the grass shoulder chatting while they waited for fares. When Sam stuck his hand up, a taxi jumped the line and pulled in to where he was standing.

The ride back into town was brief and uneventful until they got into the outskirts of the city. The driver braked suddenly, and turned into an alley. Before Sam could protest, the driver had skidded to a stop. A man with a bandana over his face pulled open Sam's door and grabbed him. The masked man mistook Sam for a frail senior. As he was pulled from the car, Sam kneed the man in the groin and shoved him to the ground. Before he could recover Sam had pulled a pepper-spray pen from his inside pocket and blasted him in the face. He whirled and caught the driver with another blast as he came at him with a club. Both men were temporarily blinded, doubled up on the road moaning in pain.

"If you think you're gonna make me miss my tee time tomorrow morning, think again," Sam told the men he'd disabled, and walked out to the street to find a friendlier taxi.

XVII

RISK

It didn't make sense that the sun was out, the wind was around five knots, that the crew was in shorts and light jackets, that the biggest heads'l was up, and that *All American* was sliding along sedately at six knots. This was the Southern Ocean, an open swath of water encircling the globe between the Antarctic and the southernmost headlands of South America, Africa, and Australia, where the wind blows a gale most of the time. The wind blows a gale here because the Southern Ocean girdles the planet unimpeded. The temperature decreases as one moves southward, and air is pulled toward the poles by the earth's rotation, causing strong westerly winds. Without any land masses blocking the 20,000-mile-long ring of water that is the Southern Ocean, the prevailing westerlies also kick up frighteningly large, menacing seas. And being bordered on the south side by the polar region, it's usually quite cold. Blizzards can happen. This ocean has acquired nicknames that shiver the timbers of anyone who has sailed there, that get the attention of anyone who is even imagining being there; nicknames like "The Roaring Forties," and "The Furious Fifties," after the degrees of latitude that define the Southern Ocean.

Roaring. Furious. That's the Southern Ocean.

But this day the crew of *All American* could have been in more sublime climes, except for one thing: the enormous iceberg off to starboard about a mile away. It was mesmerizing, a stark white island of ice brushed with bluish shadows, glistening in the bright sun. It was a mesa of ice, maybe sixty to seventy feet high, but it had to be half a mile long. As large as it was, there was three or four times more of it underwater. So they said, but that was quite impossible to imagine.

The boat was quiet. The crew was transfixed by the immensity of the berg. The boys were quietly lost in their own thoughts. Most of the off watch was on deck, some taking pictures, all eager to fully experience what for most of them was their first iceberg. Ice was one of the lurking dangers on this leg. The large bergs would appear on radar, but the smaller ones, "bergy bits," and "growlers" the size of Volkswagen Beetles that floated very low in the water, presented a perilous minefield for the race boats. Sharp eyes front were required at all times. At the press conference before the start of this 7,500-mile leg from Punta del Este to Fremantle, Western Australia, one awkward question had been how skippers planned to avoid growlers after dark. Jan

Sargent had broken the moody silence that ensued by telling the press growlers didn't come out at night.

Off watch, Andy had stretched out on the foredeck in the warm sun and had been studying the big berg with his pocket scope. Before long he found himself in the emergency rubber boat that was required equipment for all yachts in the race. It hadn't taken him long to convince Sargent it would be a good idea. *All American* had slowed to a crawl, and with the little four-horse Honda, the rubber boat would get to the berg for a quick look long before *All American* arrived. And it would be a good test of the rubber boat. Joe Dugan was with him, steering while Andy continued to focus his scope on the berg. He was fascinated by an odd play of light on shadowy areas of the ice that seemed to be coming from within the berg. Andy found himself telling Dugan about his email astronomy pal and the unidentified object in outer space they had been watching, and how his pal was convinced if an alien craft came to earth it would land in the ocean. Why look for isolated land sites when the ocean was so vast, so uninhabited? He told Joe his pal was also convinced an iceberg would be the perfect place for aliens to hide undetected.

They reached the berg in ten minutes. *All American* looked tiny behind them. They quickly spied a flat ledge that made for easy access. Their little Danforth anchor took a good bite in the ice. They tied a second line to an icy outcropping. They found a path to a larger ledge twenty feet up, and from there a steep but manageable slope to the top. Andy was taking in the incredible view of the not-so-furious Southern Ocean on this very rare, peaceful day when Joe called to him. Joe was on his knees, staring into a section of ice that was very smooth and translucent, looking like it had been melted and refrozen. Andy joined him, and was shocked by what had gotten Joe's attention: a metal surface below the surface of the ice. It was unmistakable, but what was it, a ship trapped in the ice? An airplane? A space capsule?

The sudden buzzing coming from the ice was also unmistakable. An electronic, female voice made them jump. Andy and Joe whirled around to see a voluptuous blonde in a bikini standing there holding a six-pack of beer in each hand. Her voice had a metallic ring to it as she repeated advertising clichés that weren't quite right. The lip-synch was off. The beer in one hand was labeled "Bub Lite."

Moving slowly, Joe scooped up some sun-softened ice and molded it into a ball that he threw at the blonde. It passed right through her. Andy and Joe scrambled as one, falling and sliding down the slope to their boat. The buzzing was louder. They felt the berg move under their feet. It was going to capsize . . . "ANDY! For chrissakes wake the hell up, we've got a weather system coming, all hands, man, all hands. Get dressed. Hurry it up!"

Andy was yanked out of his perilous dream with a start by Sargent yelling at him. From scrambling down the berg of his dream he was scrambling down the deck, trying to get his bearings. He didn't know which was worse, the dream or the reality.

That thought occurred to him again an hour later when he was steering *All American*, surfing downwind under spinnaker. The weather had closed in. It was very dark for midday. Visibility was limited by the strong westerly storm bearing occasional flurries of snow. Boat speed was constantly approaching thirty knots. The boat was on a tear like a big, terrified dog trying to shake its leash, challenging its master to maintain control. It was dangerous, exhilarating sailing, on the edge. At the bottom of some waves, the wind would decrease and the boat would overtake the spinnaker, causing it to collapse, then fill with a loud CRACK! as it climbed up the next hill. The acceleration could knock a person off his feet. When the boat began planing down the front of a wave, a thin vertical column of water about three feet high would shoot up on either side of the bow, close to the stem. Andy had made a note to ask Gibb Frey what that was all about. For the helmsman, it was a signal the afterburners had been lit. After those little geysers appeared, the wheel would begin to feel light in Andy's hands — light with very fine control — as he watched the speedo climb quickly to twenty-six, twenty-eight, often touching thirty knots, as he felt the boat begin to hum like a well-balanced flywheel as it tried to free itself from the sea and enter a performance zone beyond any computerized eventuality. During these mad drops down the faces of waves in the forty-foot range, Andy wondered how much of the bow section was out of the water. He wished he could see themselves. It was some ultimate, terrifying thrill. He knew how surfers must feel when they managed to catch a monster. He understood how the underlying fear increased the insatiable need to do it again, and again.

The monsters were willing. Hundreds, thousands of them were lining up to take their shots at those who would trespass upon their province. The Southern Ocean seas have a distinctive quality. They don't have just white-caps or breaking sections on their crests. Southern Ocean waves are laced with streaks of foam raised by the wind, foam turned a grayish white by the dark, blackish-blue hue of the water in these latitudes. On a good day, the water looks heavy, thick, somehow reassuring. Add thick gray clouds to take away the sun, add that layer of menacing foam streaks like the web of some hungry maritime spider, and it looks as dangerous as it is.

The danger had to be evaluated, had to be responsibly inserted into the crew's race mentality. That was easier said than done. The race mentality had been a pre-existing condition with every member of the crew with the possible exception of Andy, who had been shanghaied. But Andy was a competitor. Once he had yielded to the inevitable, it hadn't taken much to bring him into the game. Being in race mode was essential. It was also risky. Risk was part of racing, necessary for winning, but it was also an attitude that could easily become addictive and go beyond reason. The tail — the boat in this case — could easily start wagging the dog if cool heads didn't prevail. The several radio reports of trouble in the fleet, a broken rudder here, a broken boom there, helped those cooler heads (Sargent, Dimaris) with their soul-searching, helped remind them that you can't win if you don't finish. The broach put the icing on that cake.

Stu Samuels hadn't been on the wheel for five minutes when a cross wave smacked the weather (starboard) stern of *All American* about the same time those little geysers began appearing at the bow. It was very bad timing. Stu reacted quickly but the rudder was useless. There was nothing he could do but shout a warning and hang on as the boat went into a rapid right-hand turn, the lee rail rolling down hard as the spinnaker (now pulling sideways) hauled the mast toward the water. Very quickly the boat was on its ear, stopped, with the mast nearly parallel with the sea, held down by a spinnaker full of wind that was also filling with water.

Below, no one had been sleeping very hard in the heavy conditions, and all were still dressed. Stu's shout had given them a moment to react. There would be bruises aplenty, but nothing serious. Dave Zimmer fetched up covered with a pudding Teddy Bosworth had made as a dessert, something Bosworth would never let him forget.

On deck it was different. Andy and Caskie Kolegeri had grabbed winches and were hanging on, suspended, struggling to find a foothold. Stu clung to the wheel. RD had hold of the weather backstay, and Joe Dugan had fetched up on the hydraulic boom vang connecting the boom to the base of the mast.

The spinnaker had to be freed, or they would have to wait many minutes hoping it would tear apart, releasing the wind and water that was pinning them down. The boat's bottom was now broadside to the big seas that were breaking on it, sending cascades of water pouring down on the crewmen trying to hang on. They were all clipped on, but being randomly dragged by their safety harnesses was to be avoided if at all possible.

The spinnaker sheet was underwater on the leeward winch, unavailable. Andy realized his handhold was the winch holding the guy, the line to the pole end of the spinnaker. One of his flailing feet finally found a purchase on the end of the traveler track that was now vertical. He removed his left hand from the winch and found the knife he always had strapped to his leg when on deck. He lunged and reached with all he had, scraping the knife edge across the guy. The line was under such extreme tension it exploded, releasing and emptying the spinnaker, and allowing the boat to slowly but surely right itself. With one end untethered, as the mast came upright the spinnaker began tearing itself to shreds.

Stu was on it, teasing the boat back to course as water drained slowly off the deck and out of the cockpit. It didn't help that a few waves broke over the stern until speed was reached. All hands were on deck, counting heads and checking for damage to gear and themselves. The mainsail and boom were miraculously in one piece. So was the crew, freezing cold and drenched, but all accounted for. The spinnaker remains were quickly lowered and corralled thanks to the sheet staying secured to the sail. Sargent called for the number-three jib to be raised for balance. Soon *All American* was on her way to Fremantle again, making twenty knots instead of thirty. "We have found out," Sargent said to his battered crew, "when it is unadvisable to set the spinnaker."

The off watch went below to clean up the mess. Teddy Bosworth stuck his head up the hatch. "Just in case you think we dodged a bullet," the unhappy Bosworth announced, "there will be no pudding for dessert."

On the Long Island estate, Deedee was in her bedroom, where she was spending most of her time these days.

It had been a progression. First she had stopped driving and doing errands. Then she had confined herself to the house. The last time she'd gone sailing was with Andy the day he'd come to beg her to get him off The Race. That was a year ago now. For the last few months, she'd confined herself to her bedroom, an elegant suite to be sure, with its writing table, music system, television, plenty of comfortable chairs, gorgeously appointed bathroom with heated floor, walk-in closet, and a view of the boathouse and sound. But it was still the bedroom. Deedee's hairdresser came by once a week to do her hair. Myrtle did the shopping, cooking, and everything else. Myrtle brought meals that went mostly uneaten to the bedroom. It had become rare to see Deedee in any other part of the house.

It was after nine p.m. In dressing gown and robe, Deedee was at her writing desk folding papers and putting them in envelopes that she placed in a handsome wooden box that Ossie had made for her. She fastened the box shut and was trying to tie it with a ribbon when Myrtle appeared to say that Mr. Thomas wanted to know if she was ready for her evening cocktail.

"Myrtle, my hands seem to be failing me, could you tie this please?"

Myrtle tied a bow on the box. Deedee took the box and put it in a shopping bag. She covered it with a pashmina.

"Now I need you to deliver this to Becky Cotton. Just like this. Keep it out of sight. You must hand it to Becky personally, you know where her studio is, it's for her birthday."

"Yes ma'am, I know the place."

"And tell my husband yes, I'm ready for my cocktail."

Myrtle left with the box. Deedee slipped off her robe and got into bed with her back against the wedge pillow she used for reading, smoothing the covers around her. Her frail frame hardly made a bulge in the bedclothes.

Mitch arrived with her drink and some papers on a silver tray. "I brought some faxes from Race Headquarters," Mitch said. "They seem to be doing well again on leg two. Had some heavy weather, but all survived, no damage. Andy got high marks. A good article about the fashion show in Punta."

Deedee gave Mitch a close look as she took the drink and the faxes. She hadn't seen him so outgoing for some time. And saying something positive about Andy. Remarkable. Mitch could be quite charming, disarmingly so, when he needed to be. She knew that. Charming was probably the major secret of his success, in the early days anyway. Charming and opportunistic had certainly been a winning combination with her father. But as Mitch had climbed up the ranks, charming Mitch had been committed like a psychopath by mean and nasty Mitch, the real Mitch. Occasionally, the charmer got let out briefly when it was needed.

"Thanks, Mitch," Deedee said, taking a sip of her drink. "Very nice. A little . . . sweet." Deedee smiled. "Oh, I can't wait to read these."

"I'll let you be," Mitch said, turning to leave. "Sleep well."

XVIII

LIMBO

Andy was stretched out on his bunk, drifting in a semi-conscious state as a result of some crazy drug Sargent had said would relax him. It had relaxed him, all right. Knocked him right out. He'd gotten the fax several hours ago and it was still a bolt out of the blue. Deedee was dead. Not much else. The message was in formal language, like a lawyer had written it. Signed by Mitch. Deedee had "passed away peacefully" in her sleep. Period. Died? Really?! My mother?

Andy had been stunned, devastated, then enraged by the cold tone of the note, an electronic message sent to her son who was floating around on a boat a thousand miles from nowhere, already detached from social reality, in limbo. Andy had never quite gotten used to the remoteness of being on board a small boat in the open ocean. The impossibility to respond to a dire circumstance, the inability to get somewhere when he was needed, had turned remoteness into frustration resembling torture. First the Mountain View debacle, now this, Deedee, his mother, the only real foundation in his otherwise untethered life. His mother who really loved him. Gone. He knew she wasn't in great shape. He knew she had given in to what seemed to him like minor ailments, and okay, she was an alcoholic, but hell, a well-paced, functional alcoholic like her could live to be a hundred.

Andy didn't have much experience where death was concerned. He'd been just a kid when his grandfather had died. That had been a big deal, with many hundreds at the funeral. He'd been sad because, well, it was a sad event. And his grandfather had paid attention to him. He never imagined the old man loved him. He was just interested in him, like Andy was a science project, some lab animal on two feet. But it was attention, and the old man had such cool stuff, boats, bicycles, strange scientific tools and devices, and most of all the big telescope, the ticket to the universe in all its amazing grandeur. It had hooked Andy big time, and he was grateful for that. The funeral did its thing. There were tears everywhere. The sadness was contagious. A few other relatives and acquaintances of Andy's had died, but as for death causing deep, personal trauma, this was a first.

Being on a sixty-footer with eleven other people, there was no solitude. He was a mess, alternately overcome with grief and disgusted with the way he had been informed; disgusted with his situation, his life. Grief-stricken and disgusted. That was when Sargent and Joe Dugan had unlocked the boat's medical kit and produced the relaxant. Both of them had tried to be helpful. Andy had been raving about getting a helicopter to lift him off so he could fly home. Joe had sat with him while the drug was taking charge, good old practical Joe Dugan telling him they were hundreds of miles out of Fremantle, first of all, beyond helicopter range, and there'd be nothing for him to do if he were home, nothing but probably get his ass in trouble, or get drunk, cause a scene, wreck a car, get ugly with Mitch. Maybe Joe was making sense, but sense was temporarily an unavailable concept for Andy. We're talking about death, Andy thought, gone forever . . . how much freaking sense does that make?

Sargent made Dugan's practicality seem mild. Sargent always went right for the core. The last thing Andy had heard before the drug took over was Sargent saying it wasn't going to change. The sooner Andy figured out how to live with it, the better off he would be. "You are where you are and there's nothing to be done about that," Sargent had said to him. "Do your job. Deedee wanted you on this race. Make her proud." Sargent had a nasty habit of being right.

"Welcome back." It was Joe Dugan, ever watchful. "How'd that work? Seems to have put you right out."

"Big time." Andy stretched, rubbed his eyes. Joe gave him some water. "My mother died, right? That wasn't just a bad trip?"

"Right."

"How long I been out?"

Joe looked at his watch. "About eight hours."

"No other faxes?"

"Nope."

Andy was quiet, took another slug of water. "That stuff dries you out."

"Yes it does. Feel okay?"

"Yeah. Where are we? What's up?"

"Been quiet. But we're closing on Fremantle. A few hundred miles. We think *Ram Bunctious* is nearby."

"That could be fun."

"Jan is cranked."

Andy got up, stretched, walked to the navigation station, sat down, and began catching up. It was noon, not twelve o'clock p.m. Astronomers know that noon marks that moment when half the day's light has passed, whether it's twelve o'clock p.m. or not. The boat was close reaching in ten knots of wind. The biggest heads'l was up. The watch was paying attention, but relaxed, chatting quietly.

Andy studied the chart. From following the twelve-meter world championships in 1986, prior to the America's Cup in 1987, Andy knew about the so-called Fremantle Doctor, the strong onshore breeze that comes up most afternoons off Fremantle. He wondered how many miles west of Fremantle the Doctor could be felt. He started poring over the latest weather faxes. The southeasterly breeze being directed along the coast of the Australian Bight was giving them the tight reach they were on. It was early yet, but Andy could see indications of it already starting to clock toward the south about seventy miles out. He'd watch it.

"Sail!" It was BN who spotted *Ram Bunctious*. The boat was a dot on the horizon, barely visible to the north, a good ten miles away. After racing across nearly 7,500 miles of open ocean, there she was. Unbelievable.

"Okay," Sargent said from the wheel. "Now we pay attention. I want my case of rum back."

The watch changed in half an hour. Andy was up, but he asked Stu if he minded taking the helm, he wanted to look at the navigation. He had an idea. "Really? Me?" Stu said. "I can't believe you want to give up a wheel watch that's going to be so much fun." Andy had to smile as he went below. The wind had increased, pushing twenty knots. They had changed down to the number-two jib and remained on a tight reach, on course for Fremantle. Seas were up just enough to make it rough going. Both Andy and Stu enjoyed the challenge of what was probably the most difficult point of sailing in anything over fifteen knots. Hard on the wind the helmsman could always feather up in the gusts to ease pressure on sails and rig. On a broader reach he had the option to head down in the puffs. Close reaching was more of a lock when you wanted to maximize speed. Because course changes were minimized, having hands on the main sheet and traveler were critical. The steering priority in those conditions was finding a path through an obstacle course of building waves that were about forty-five degrees to the bow. A little ease on traveler and sheet in the right combination and at the right moment made steering a team effort. A good helmsman anticipates. On a tight reach in eighteen to twenty knots, three people have to anticipate. If the main and traveler trimmers were to wait for the helmsman's call, it would be too late. Plus, those two have to work together: traveler down first, then ease the main as necessary. It helped to have another pair of eyes looking to weather, calling the puffs. Caskie Kolegeri was very good at it. And Caskie was there to trim when needed.

Andy was back on deck in thirty minutes. Sargent and navigator Peter Dimaris came up with him. "Andy's got a plan," Sargent said. "Peter and I think we like it."

"There's the Fremantle Doctor," Andy said, "a strong westerly that comes up off Fremantle most afternoons. Land heats up, cold ocean wind blows onshore. The question is, how far offshore does that effect start? Fifty miles, a hundred? We're around a hundred out and we haven't felt it yet. But with *Ram* close, every second will count. We need to get the spinnaker on deck ready to hoist the minute we sense this shift."

"You're counting on this shift coming from the right?" It was Davis.

"Yes, it should come from the right."

"How so?"

"I've looked at the way the southerly whips around the southwest corner of Australia," Andy said. "There's nothing in the meteorological history to suggest that trend could be reversed when that's the situation. Plus it's gonna be a hot day in Fremantle. The Doctor is just waiting to make a house call."

Davis shrugged.

Andy listened to himself and was surprised. The guy who had once tried moving heaven and earth not to go on this insane race was suddenly taking charge, sticking his neck out? What the hell! But he was into it. He suddenly felt strong.

"Here's what I think we should do," Andy said. "When we feel the wind starting to shift, we'll come off ten to fifteen degrees and set the chute. That will put us below course. That's okay because the idea is to stay close to *Ram*."

"Think we can cross them?" Crouse asked.

"We've got about a half mile lead," Dimaris said. "Should be enough with the spinnaker."

"We don't want to be sailing in different water and let luck decide who wins this leg," Andy said. "We also want to get to leeward of them. When the sou'westerly fills behind us we'll come back to course and we'll have a faster sailing angle to the finish. With fifty to sixty miles to go, that will give us enough runway. And we should put some distance on them before they can set."

"It sounds dicey," Davis said.

"Andy makes sense," Sargent said. "We may have a slight lead, but right now *Ram* has that leeward advantage. When, and if" — he smiled — "the Doctor fills, I agree that advantage will be critical. If the Doctor gets a flat tire, well, Andy can buy the rum this time."

"Done deal. Organize the chute for a port set," Andy said. "When the shift starts, we'll have to go with it. We'll be low of course for a while, but we have to believe it will settle in, come west, get behind us."

"Let's get that red top reacher on deck," Sargent said. "Make sure it's in stops. Stu, you or Andy will be the first to feel the shift. Sing out. We'll want all hands on this one. Roger, you and Joe walk it through. I know you know. A hundred times. Make it a hundred and one. Get Zimmer and Crouse on deck when you want them to handle sheet and guy. Larry and Bosworth can get the jib down. Caskie's on the handles."

An hour later, Andy was steering when he felt it. The breeze began shifting right, clocking ever so slightly, as he'd predicted. *Ram* was off to the left about four miles, keeping pace. *All American* was maintaining its slight lead. One could have fired shotguns and the crew on the other boat wouldn't have heard them, but Andy kept his voice down just in case. "Here it comes," Andy said to RD, who was on the main. Davis had already eased a few inches. Stu had eased the jib. "Get everybody up."

Ten minutes later both sails had been eased even more. The wind was on the beam. All hands were on deck. Sargent nodded at Andy. This was his party.

RD and Joe Dugan set the pole, then hauled red top to the masthead. Davis returned to the main, ready to ease. Dugan was on the jib. Zimmer had the spinnaker sheet in hand with three wraps on the big winch drum. Caskie was crouched over the grinder, feet spread, hands clutching the handles. The crew felt like an NFL offensive unit in the red zone, poised, set, ready for the snap.

"Coming off," Andy said quietly. "Five degrees, ten . . . Break it!"

RD eased the main sheet as Andy drove off. Caskie spun the handles. The spinnaker opened at the foot and the thirty stops exploded nearly as one as the chute filled with a loud pop. Andy put the wheel down as the chute heeled the boat twenty-five degrees. Dugan was at the mast casting off the jib halyard. Down it came with Teddy Bosworth and Larry Kolegeri seated on the deck to corral the quarrelsome sail. The boat's acceleration was fierce. The chute was worth at least three knots of speed. The pole had been perfectly set, low and way forward. "Stop!" Zimmer said to Caskie, and eased some sheet.

For thirty minutes Andy held the course that was now ten to fifteen degrees below where they wanted to go. They crossed *Ram*, which was holding a proper course for Fremantle, now reaching under a big jib. *Ram* had been off their left hip. Soon she was off their right hip. Sargent was still in the cockpit, saying nothing, but his poker face was studied, fighting off doubt. Doubt was also beginning to cramp Andy's enthusiasm. He was stealing still another anxious glance at *Ram*, now half a mile to windward and looking slightly ahead, just as Zimmer broke the silence with a simple little statement that brought joy: "You can come up."

Both the wind instruments and the mast head fly showed the wind now trending slightly aft of the beam. Andy steered up five degrees and the boat took it. It was a fact, they were starting to feel the Doctor that was clocking more, letting them slowly but surely come back up to course for Fremantle as Andy had figured. They were back up ten. Dimaris kept putting the bearing compass on *Ram*. After ten minutes he smiled. "We're faster," Peter said.

They could see the action on *Ram*'s deck as that crew felt the shift and hustled to set the spinnaker. Soon *Ram*'s big sail was up and pulling. But *All American*'s better angle to the finish was worth almost a knot of boat speed. Not that it wasn't on the hairy side. The speedo was in the seventeen-to-eighteen-knot range. The lee rail was down, with the crew packed on the high-side rail. Watches had been cancelled. Sargent had tersely pointed out they could sleep tomorrow.

The foot of the chute dipped occasionally and so did the main boom that was being eased by Davis in the puffs. But Stu remarked how stable the helm felt when he took over. Everything was on edge, right where a race boat likes it. Two hours later they had what looked like a half-mile lead on *Ram Bunctious*. As the Doctor settled in from the sou'west, they changed to a spinnaker cut for sailing deeper downwind, and held their lead to the finish, winning by six minutes and change.

Andy's back tingled from the pounding it took from his ecstatic crewmates. "What was in that drug you gave him?" Teddy Bosworth asked Dugan.

Andy slipped below during the cleanup on deck, suddenly exhausted. He slumped into Peter's Recaro seat at the nav table and closed his eyes, opening a widescreen shot of Deedee hammering home that unreturnable backhand. In the acrid, wet, below-decks mess of a round-the-world race boat at the end of a brutal Southern Ocean leg, Andy Thomas put his head on the nav table and cried his heart out.

A light snow was falling as Andy stood contemplating Deedee's grave at the private cemetery located on the outskirts of his family's thousand-acre estate. He'd come directly from the airport after the twenty-hour trek from Western Australia. He was right to assume Mitch would have had Deedee put in the ground as soon as possible. The dirt was freshly disturbed around the grave site, full of footprints being painted by the snow flurry. Probably no ceremony. That would have been his mother's wish, and Mitch's convenience. He placed the bunch of flowers he'd picked up at the airport on the grave — there was no headstone yet — stood back and appreciated the view of Long Island Sound in the distance, across big fields where corn would grow in summer. He hadn't been to the family cemetery in many years and had forgotten what a peaceful spot it was. Deedee will like it here, he thought, and realized how ridiculous that sounded, right out of a sentiment by Hallmark. The celebration, the ritual of death is all about the living who support the business for their own satisfaction. The dead couldn't care less. I like it here, he thought, and that's what matters because now I will think of this expansive, pastoral scene when I think of my mother, and that's calming. For me. Andy had to smile at how Sargent would approve of his attitude even as he wiped away a tear with his gloved hand.

Sargent. The race. That wild finish, sailing into the Doctor, going after *Ram Bunctious*, setting the spinnaker early, heading off to nail down the leeward position, that faster angle . . . Altogether an insane bit really, but it worked, damned if it hadn't worked! The race. The bloody race. "You win," Andy said quietly to his mother. "You win, and so did I."

The approaching car caught Andy's attention. Only family and good friends knew about the seldom-used dirt road into the cemetery. It was a Subaru hatchback, definitely not Mitch's, thank heaven. Andy wasn't at all interested in seeing Mitch. Maybe Ossie? The car stopped and Becky Cotton got out. Her big dog jumped out and ran toward Andy. He was a Belgian Malinois, a good eighty pounds, like a German shepherd only more streamlined.

The Malinois is powerful, fast, and smart, a favorite of the military and the police. Andy had met him a few times when Sam had brought him to the office. Gus, he remembered. "Gus!" The dog reacted, skidded to a halt at his feet, and sat down expectantly. Andy showed respect, reached out slowly, stroked his head.

"What about me?" Becky had her hands on her hips.

"Shall we just cut to the chase?" Andy asked.

"Yes, we should." Becky's signal to Gus was subtle.

Their hug was passionate, prolonged. They kissed and it was wonderfully electric, just as Andy remembered it. Gus made a wistful sound in his throat. They laughed.

"There's a lot to catch up on," Becky said. "I'm so glad you're here . . . I mean I'm sorry you have to be here of course . . . I couldn't get to Punta, I just couldn't . . . "

"It's okay."

"I know all about Mountain View, I've been helping Dad figure it out. I got my law degree, you know, before I decided to do photography full time."

"I know Mitch is in charge," Andy said, "but it's okay, I'm not broke." Andy pulled the bloodstained ten-thousand-peso bill from his pocket.

"There's a lot you don't know."

"I know I'm cold."

Becky laughed. "Me too. Let's go to Dad's cabin. It's only half an hour or so from here. Things aren't as you imagine."

XIX

SECRETS

Andy had dozed off. Becky shifted in his arms, waking him.

"Wow." Andy was still in another world, his first visit to that place where love and the convergence of souls reduce the speed of light to a crawl, creating a weightless, delirious limbo, and providing a momentary hallelujah glimpse of all things perfect. Organ music, full stops. He was still suspended, just starting to feel gravity reclaiming him. His mind felt the way fingers prickle after being sleep-bound.

"Spectacular," Becky whispered in his ear.

"You knew."

"Yes, so did you, I'll bet."

"I have to admit . . . "

"That's why, well, there's a lot of important stuff, but this, I mean, priorities are so vital."

"We had to finish what we started fifteen years ago," Andy said.

"That would be twelve years . . . "

"And how many days?"

Becky laughed. "Thirty-four days and — what time is it — fourteen hours."

"Really?!"

"You bet." She laughed.

Becky slipped out of bed and stretched, pulling her hair back. Andy couldn't believe the extraordinary view, the beauty. "Come on, get dressed," she said. "Lots to do." She opened the door and gave a signal. Gus dashed in and jumped on the bed, licking Andy's face. A lot of animal, Andy thought. Formidable. Lucky he's willing to share.

Andy loved Sam Cotton's cabin. It was very basic, a hunting and fishing camp that reflected Sam's nature. It was small, with a large mud and laundry room off a living room/kitchen that was built around a fireplace in which a proper woodstove had been installed. There was Sam's bedroom, which Andy now had a fondness for, and across the hall a bunkroom for Sam's buddies. Both bathrooms had a drain in the middle of the floor for easy cleaning. Oil-filled radiators kept those rooms warm.

The cabin was one of five that had been built on a hilly, wooded island of about a thousand acres surrounded by a confusion of tidal streams, creeks, and channels leading to Long Island Sound. Gus flopped down on his bed next to the woodstove. Andy set up a teepee of the dry kindling Sam kept handy, and torched it off while Becky was making tea. Then he studied the map of the area pinned to the wall in the kitchen. A path was indicated leading from the house a hundred yards or so through woods and scrub to a boathouse. The four other camps on the island were indicated. Blinds for hunting were noted by pushpins. There were inked notations in various colors.

"The colors indicate seasonal bird activity," Becky said, joining Andy at the map. "Ducks — coots, mergansers — are in red. Scaup are blue, snow geese green, brants are brown. I can't imagine shooting a snow goose. They are so pretty. You've seen them circling in the midday sun, the way the light keeps changing. Gorgeous. It's a crazy place. Getting out to the sound is like running a maze. Some of the channels dry up at really low tides. And they change. The other cottages out here are closed up by now. Only my father keeps his place going all winter. He loves it here year-round."

"No kidding. Why haven't I ever been here?"

"Too busy, I suppose." Becky gave him a look, then a smile.

She went to the side table and picked up the box Myrtle had delivered to her. It was the size of a shoebox, varnished teak and holly, with dovetailed corners and brass hardware. An art piece. She put it on the kitchen table.

"Handsome," Andy said, his fingers caressing the finish.

"Ossie's work."

"I could have guessed."

"Myrtle delivered it to me the day after Deedee died."

"You know what's inside?"

"I've seen and read everything, Sam's read it. He's the executor of the estate."

"He told me that in Punta. He said I'd better be nice to him."

"You'd better."

Andy had to admire his mother's organization. It felt good that the box had been previewed, and that Becky was so comfortable about urging him to open it, so he did. Two envelopes were on top. One addressed in Deedee's unmistakable shaky but formal hand to Sam and Becky, and one to him and Becky. Both had been opened.

"Huh," Andy said. "So much for personal and confidential."

"Hey, my name is on it too. She wanted it all on the table," Becky said. "You can read Sam's and my letter, but it's mostly legal details you can pore over later. Read ours."

Andy sat down and opened the envelope. Becky brought him a mug of tea, then watched him squint at the handwriting.

"I'll read it if you wish. I know it by heart."

Andy handed her the letter.

"First she says she wrote it by hand so there would be no mistake about its authenticity. Then it goes on: 'For some months I have known I have cancer of the pancreas, stage four. I have a few months left. Only Myrtle and I know this, and the doctor of course, not that it would matter to Mitch, whom I am certain is trying to end my life. My green medicine has had a distinctly sweet taste of late. If only he knew he needn't bother. It's my little surprise for him.'"

"Damn, are you kidding? Christ, could she be right?"

"There's more: 'The woman Mitch is currently seeing is called Isha . . .'"

"Stop!"

Andy's head was in his hands, eyes closed, the better to take in this onslaught of information, the better to speed-scan cloudy images of oh-so-subtle glances here and there between Mitch and Isha at dinners and cocktail parties at the club, split-second glimpses of touches that he ignored at the time or passed off as totally innocent, or maybe just letchy, under the influence of too many drinks. But it made sense. It definitely made sense. Two of a kind for chrissakes. Another puzzle piece. He knew Mitch had always had women on the side. Everybody knew, Deedee included. But Isha? Whew. Blind. Then again, when Isha had come along he had been blind most of the time, totally pissed about everything, pissed from drinking all the time, just carrying on the family tradition, his mother's side. Isha was suddenly there for the taking, and that wasn't all bad. She liked the money of course, but exactly why she had shown up, or who she was, had never occurred to him. But Mitch? Ho boy.

"Okay."

"'But I am at peace,'" Becky continued reading. "'There are facts you should know. Mitch is not your biological father. I probably should have told you this long ago, but I try not to regret that decision. Your well-being was always first in my heart. Your real father is a man named Grady Smith, a New Zealander who was my father's boat captain. How I loved Grady. He was living in Australia when I last heard. When I became pregnant,

Father was outraged. He was embarrassed! What would people think . . . of him! Abortion was out of the question. Me marrying a lowly boat captain was out of the question for Randolph Moss. Instead, he threatened Grady, sent him away, and arranged for Mitch, his ambitious protégé at Moss, to be the acceptable father of my unborn child.'"

Andy held up his hand for Becky to stop. He got up and walked unsteadily to the window, eyes brimming with tears. He turned to Becky. "It must be Christmas," he said, "because I've received two amazing presents today. Now I learn Mitch is not my fucking father, oh my God, can you believe that? I must have known inside, all these years, I must have known. I knew! I did."

"I knew you would like that part," Becky said, going to him and laying a hug on him that rang bells and made him feel like he was in the clouds.

"Sit. There's more."

Andy sat down carefully. "Old Randolph," he said. "What a consummate bastard. What a paranoid fool, what a son of a bitch. Pathetic. Can you imagine doing that to your daughter? You know, she told me he called her to his bedside when he was dying, told her he was leaving her everything, everything except what she wanted most — his recognition of her talent, her ability. You know why? Because he didn't want her to think for a minute she was as good as he. On his deathbed that narcissistic, mad genius reached out and severely damaged her. His dispatching of Grady Smith had to be a terrible blow. Mean. Cruel. Unforgivable. And Mitch! Randolph could really pick 'em. But when her own, beloved dad told her she wasn't worthy, that's what really crippled her."

"Listen." Becky read on: "'For years Sam has thought Mitch was trying to harm you. I never agreed with him until lately. He told me about being attacked in the taxi in Punta del Este. Now I fear I might have sent you to your death on The Race."

Andy had his head in his hands again. He was in free fall, running more tapes, the gunshot in the tunnel — that was for him? — that ugly meeting in Mitch's office about The Race, harassment on the boulders at Outward Bound, nearly going over the side during the first leg, the Knife Man and his meeting with Isha . . . Finally, he was putting it together with growing trepidation that made him feel claustrophobic.

"Sam was attacked? In a taxi?! . . . "

"You didn't know? How could you. It was after the fashion show. Dad grabbed a cab to the hotel. It turned into an alley, and this guy and the driver came at him."

"He must be okay or we'd be at the hospital."

"He maced them. Left them both mewling on the ground. He carries these little mace pens, pepper spray, has for years. We've always kidded him about them."

Andy laughed out loud. "Sam. Jesus. Did he call the cops?"

"No, he just wanted to get to his hotel. He had a golf date the next morning and a plane that afternoon. He was anxious to get to bed. He's eighty, don't forget. He thought it was just, you know, locals having a go at a 'rich American.' It didn't occur to him until it was too late that the thugs might have been commissioned."

"Who has control after Sam?"

"I do."

"So I'd better be nice."

"Right."

"And you'd better be careful. If he went after Sam . . . "

"I know."

Andy sat down at the table. He and Becky looked at each other over Ossie's box. She looked fantastic, turtleneck, flannel shirt, hair in a hasty braid, bright-eyed. "Deedee left you everything," Becky said. "Full ownership of Moss Optics. The property. Everything. I guess that would include the race boat." She smiled.

Andy wasn't smiling. "It's dangerous right now. Feels like Mitch is closing in, trying to cash in big time, expand the deal he made with Randolph nearly thirty years ago, turn it into his personal bonanza. He wants it all. It's coming together. And Sam, you, me, we're in the way. I don't know the details, but Mitch has a plan. He's got to be behind the Mountain View catastrophe."

"Sam is sure of it. Just another way of discrediting you, trying to break you. We'll know soon enough. I'm told we now know where your man George Cooper went to ground. Somewhere in Malaysia."

"Malaysia!"

"They'll find him."

"So stupid." Andy paced. "You know who introduced me to him? Jeff reminded me. Isha!"

Becky shook her head. "That's what happens when you let your . . . "

"Yeah yeah, I know."

"We've got Mitch." Becky pulled a photograph from the box and handed it to Andy. It was a shot of an old-fashioned glass inside a plastic evidence bag. The glass was a handsome piece of crystal. Delicate. Andy recognized it as a favorite of Deedee's. "Myrtle was smart enough to pick this up, with a napkin, from Deedee's bedside table after she fell asleep the night she died. It's been to the lab. They found insulin residue in it, and Mitch's fingerprints. And, of course, Myrtle saw him deliver it."

Andy walked to the window and stared out at the fields dusted lightly with patches of snow. The tan, dead grasses and scrub beneath showed the dreary winter patina of a Wyeth landscape. The snow had stopped, but the day was gray, the temperature in the low thirties.

"Did you say all the other places out here are closed up?"

"Yes. I know because . . . "

"Expecting anyone?" Andy pulled the powerful little scope from his pocket. "Car down by the gatehouse."

"They'll need a code to get in."

"Not these guys." Andy whirled around. "We're outta here!"

"Boathouse!" Becky said, stepping into her boots, grabbing a jacket. She stuffed the letters and photo into the box, slammed it shut, and tucked it under her arm.

Pulling on his jacket, Andy took one more look toward the gatehouse. The car was moving fast along the causeway. Behind it, the broken gate was left open. "Come on," Becky said. Gus led the way out the back door. Snow was falling again and it was slippery underfoot. Becky went down but was quickly on her feet again. The path was narrowed by bushes bent down, heavy from ice and snow. They needed several minutes to get to the boathouse. It took all of Andy's strength to wrench open the door, swollen shut.

It was a small boathouse, old, solid, but like the cabin, without frills. Inside the door was a narrow deck about three feet off the water that ran the width of the building. From the deck, steps led down to floating docks. There were lifts for two boats. Sam's duckboat was on one. Becky threw on the power and flipped the switch on the other lift, which began lowering Sam's classic 1950s Chris-Craft runabout. Andy grabbed the box, then pulled himself up on the boat and began removing the cover, tearing at the cold snaps and zippers. The boat lowered down at a snail's pace, the wire cables grinding on the rollers. It was maddening. Andy didn't think they'd make it. He'd heard the dull thunk of car doors shutting. It wouldn't take the visitors long to search the cabin and pick up the foot tracks to the boathouse.

He jumped down onto the floating dock looking for a weapon. He grabbed a long wooden boat hook hanging on the wall, then took the three steps up as one. He jammed the boathouse door shut, grabbed the hunk of small line hanging from the handle, and quickly secured it around a large nail protruding from the doorjamb. He saw a bucket with a line hitched to it, lowered it into the water, and pulled up a load of water he sloshed on the deck. He positioned himself beside the door.

Becky was in the runabout before it touched the water, pumping the choke, advancing the throttle, turning the key. The motor caught, sputtered, quit. She tried again with same result. Becky turned the key and the motor cranked again as someone began pulling on the door. On the third heave, the line broke and the door flew open as the runabout's engine roared to life, belching a thick cloud of black smoke. A man dashed into the boathouse. Andy drove the boat hook between his legs. He went down hard on the wet deck and slid into the freezing water.

The second man followed quickly, pistol in hand. Andy heard Becky's low double whistle. In a flash Gus leaped and sank his teeth into the second man's wrist just as he fired. The round missed Becky, shattering the runabout's windshield. The man's weapon clattered onto the deck and bounced into the water. Struggling to release Gus's hold on him, the man howled in pain. Andy ran to the boat. Another whistle, and Gus released the attacker and leaped aboard. The boat was barely afloat, but it was enough. Becky threw it in gear, hit the throttle, and the boat slipped off the lift just as the man in the water was pulling himself up on the transom. His face contorted in agony and he screamed as the propeller cut heavily into his foot, turning the boat's wake a bad color.

Becky threw the engine into neutral after blasting out of the shed. She dug in her parka, pulled out a small camera, and grabbed a shot of the boathouse and the two men, one in the water, the other bent over on the deck. She put the boat in gear and idled ahead. Becky knew the way. She'd been running these channels with her father since childhood. Dead slow was the only way to stay afloat and weave through the narrow, barely visible channels overgrown with bushes.

"You okay?"

"Look at that windscreen," Becky said, her voice a little shaky. "Sam is gonna be very upset."

"Some dog you got." Andy scratched Gus's head.

"I shot a K9 story. Gus had broken his leg. They were

going to put him down. I took him. One of the trainers told me his commands. He wasn't supposed to. First action he's seen." Becky gave a shiver. "Me too."

"Can you get to the gatehouse?"

"There's a little duck-in before we get there."

"No big rush. They'll have to regroup."

"That's lucky."

"Nice work."

"This boat's always been a tough start."

Andy wanted these guys. He was right that it would take them a while to get moving. One of them had to be fished out of the water by a man with one good arm. Both of them would need the bleeding stopped before they could travel. If he hadn't drowned, the guy in the water had to be in shock.

Becky steered the boat slowly through the channels. Andy was baffled by how anyone could commit all the twists and turns to memory. There didn't seem to be any markers. It all looked the same to him. But in less than five minutes they had come out of the marsh bushes into a slightly wider creek that ran under the old wooden causeway bridge. No car was in sight. Becky reversed the Chris-Craft into a natural indention in the creek hardly bigger than the boat, and passed a stern line around the trunk of a bush. She cut the engine.

The gatehouse was about thirty yards away. Andy grabbed the boat hook and a ball of heavy-twist white cotton string he'd found in a dashboard compartment. Becky tucked the box under one arm. They hurried to the cover of the gatehouse. Andy dragged the bent gate back just enough so it blocked the road. They waited.

It was a good twenty minutes before the car appeared, moving fast down the hill from the cabin. It skidded to a stop in front of the gate. The driver got out. He was in obvious discomfort. Becky recognized one of Sam's scarves he'd rigged as a sling for his right arm. As the man struggled to move the gate, Andy stepped out of his cover and swung the boat hook, catching him across the forehead. By the time the man regained consciousness, his hands had been tied and he was propped up in the back seat with his sopping-wet friend, who was unconscious.

"He needs help," the man muttered as he came around.

"I think I can arrange that," Andy said. "But first, you have to do something for me. You have to call Mr. Mitchell Thomas and tell him what he wants to hear."

"I don't know any Mitchell Thomas."

Becky made a quick, low sound in her throat. Gus, who was sitting beside the car's open door, focused his attention on the man and began growling in a way that made Andy's skin crawl. The man's eyes bulged with fear.

"Okay, okay . . . "

"You blow it, pull any tricks, and I will toss you to this dog like a bone."

Hearing the anger in Andy's voice caused Gus to growl a little louder. Gus lifted his lip, showing fangs. Andy couldn't remember when he'd seen a better performance from a dog. He was full of admiration. He darted a look at Becky. Their eyes met and held like those of two singers harmonizing.

Andy produced the phone he'd taken from the man while he was unconscious. "How is he listed?"

"Boss Moss," he mumbled.

Andy dialed, held the phone to the man's mouth. Gus growled again. Becky gave him a signal and he was silent.

"Job done," the man said into the phone. Andy hung it up.

"Okay, now maybe we can find a police station on the way to the hospital. Hope you don't mind if my friend rides with you."

Gus jumped into the back seat between the two men and sat upright, looking serious.

XX

RAID

It was Andy and Becky's third night on the rooftop. It had taken some doing. At considerable risk, Jeff Linn had outmaneuvered Mitch's guard-dog secretaries and managed to find the address of his Manhattan hideaway, a penthouse apartment on the west side of Central Park. Then Jeff had broken all kinds of laws by flying a small drone over eastside rooftops across the park to find the ideal place for observation. New Yorkers living on either side of the park have long enjoyed innocent amusement by observing one another over the treetops with powerful telescopes. One of Manhattan's highest-rent districts is not immune to one of the city's oldest pastimes. It's not that people don't mind. They simply forget about it. Spying is just a part of big-city, high-rise life; nothing personal, just people-watching refined. And it's free. If one does think about it, well, he (or she) can always close the curtains. Or choose to leave them open. With the drone, Jeff had found a building directly opposite Mitch's with a flat, uncluttered roof.

Getting access to the rooftop was solved by slipping the building's doorman a couple crisp hundreds, explaining that photographer Becky needed just the right elevation and location for a night shot of Central Park. Cards and credentials were also produced. By the third night (they pleaded weather problems), the doorman was fast becoming their best friend. He even said he'd watch their car in the no-parking zone, not to worry. With Becky lugging the tripod, and Andy carrying boxes of gear, the doorman happily ferried them to the roof in the elevator.

It was ten p.m., and it was cold. A brisk northerly was putting the wind chill at around twenty-five degrees. It was also clearing the air. They tucked into the lee of a large air-conditioning unit and set up the tripod. Andy attached his Stealth Scope to the tripod for maximum stability. He opened one of the gear boxes, took out a thermos of coffee, and poured each of them a cup. From the other box he removed two folding stools. Andy stared through the scope. Becky sat down and sipped her coffee.

They had located Mitch's apartment the first night. Winter, and the absence of leaves on the tallest trees, made the job easier, but it took an actual Mitch sighting to confirm they had the right place. After that, finding the apartment was easy: top floor, the one with the big picture window framed by red draperies. The two took turns gazing through the scope for a few minutes at a time. They were one story, maybe a little more, above Mitch's floor, giving them a good view of the living-room layout. The hallway to the elevator was on the far left. The small window to the right was a bathroom. Further right was the bedroom window, also picture-size.

Andy was hoping this would be the night. Wait any longer and he was afraid the cats would be out of the bag. The thugs that had attacked them at the boathouse had been treated, and were being held under tight security. The doctors had managed to save the guy's foot. And as far as Andy knew, Mitch was unaware he had flown home. But there were all sorts of leaks possible. Sam was pretending business as usual, supposedly processing Deedee's estate. Mitch had no clue Deedee had overwritten everything, and he was pushing Sam and the other attorneys to get it done, signed, sealed, and delivered — to him. But Andy could hear the clock ticking. He had the goods, all the evidence, and it was in the right hands, no problem there. Sam had everything he needed. But sooner would be better. Andy's flight back to Western Australia was in three days. Another night without a hit would not be good.

"Contact," Becky said quietly.

"Lemme see." Andy moved to the scope, taking a split second to marvel again at the clarity this gorgeous little optic provided, along with the incredible magnification. Mitch must have been seated, maybe watching television. Out of sight. Now he was up, in frame, moving to meet someone who had just come in. Isha, in the flesh. She must have her own key. Maybe she was calling this place home while Mitch was on the island. She shed her long down coat. They hugged. Bingo! Funny, he thought, staring at the two of them, how he didn't feel so much as a twinge. If he felt anything it was a swipe of disgust with himself for being such a damn fool. He cursed under his breath.

"It's over," Becky said, catching the vibe with both hands. "Let's end it."

Andy opened the box, pulled out a radio, made a call. "Jason here."

"It's Andy. We've had a sighting. We're on if you're set."

"We're set. Meet you at the address in thirty minutes."

It took them twenty-five minutes to pack up, thank the doorman, who wondered how they could have gotten what they wanted so quickly, and drive to the other side of the park. Captain Jason was waiting in the lobby with a detective, and two young uniformed officers, a man and a woman. Jason was a Black man of linebacker proportions with a serious countenance to match. His shoulders were broad under his overcoat. His head was large, his jaw square, his eyes calm, steady. Andy noticed the doorman was quite nervous. Jason had read him the riot act, and he was being watched just in case resident loyalty moved him to make a warning call upstairs.

"Both home?" Jason asked, his voice low and even.

"Twenty-five minutes ago," Andy said.

"Good." Jason indicated to the male officer whose name tag read "Quimby" that he should stay in the lobby until they were inside, to prevent any warning calls. Andy suggested that Becky might want to wait for them in the lobby.

"Not on a bet," she said, with enough enthusiasm that Andy knew it would be pointless to argue. He was finding that everything this woman did was appealing. Jason glanced at Becky, gave Andy the slightest of nods, and the five of them took the elevator to the penthouse floor. The detective knocked politely on the apartment door, then rang the bell. Silence. He knocked again, a little stronger.

"Hello? Yes. Who is it?" It was Isha's voice.

"Police," the detective said quietly, putting additional chill on a word one doesn't want to hear outside the apartment door at eleven at night.

"Police?"

"Yes ma'am."

"Just a moment." One could hear footsteps retreating.

Jason gave it ten counts, shrugged as if to ask, where could they go? — then nodded. The detective knocked again, rang the bell.

"Yes yes, just a moment!" Isha sounded irritated. She opened the door. Jason and the detective moved in slowly but with resolve, showing their credentials. It helped they were both large men. Andy, Becky, and the female officer followed. Isha backed away. Mitchell Thomas appeared, looking both puzzled and offended by this sudden intrusion of strangers into his penthouse fortress. Both Mitch and Isha spotted Andy and Becky just as Jason spoke. Andy saw a flash of fear flit across Mitch's eyes.

"I'm Captain Victor Jason. This is detective first-class James Baker, and Officer Jones. I think you know the others. You are Mitchell Thomas?"

"Yes I am," Mitch intoned in his best command voice, making an effort to sound confident.

"Mr. Thomas, at 11:04 p.m. on November 18th, 1990, I am arresting you for the murder of Dorothy Moss Thomas, also known as Mrs. Mitchell Thomas. You have the right to remain silent. Anything you say can and will be used against you in a court of law."

Mitch stared at Jason as if he expected him to dissolve into a puff of smoke at any second. Total disbelief registered on his face. Then he managed a chuckle. "Do you know who I am?" he asked, his arrogance surfacing. "This is a joke, right? You come walking into my apartment, my home, at eleven o'clock at night and tell me I am a murderer, and more than that, that my victim is my wife?"

"Yes sir, that's about right," Jason said.

"Well you can just wait a goddamn minute because I have one call and I will make it right now to a lawyer who will make you wish you never heard my goddamn name!" Mitch was yelling, the veins standing out on his temples.

Officer Quimby arrived about then. Detective Baker had pinged him on the radio. Baker was moving to secure Mitch as Captain Jason was explaining to him that he would not be calling anyone, that he would be afforded his first call at the station, when Isha attacked Quimby. With all the focus on Mitch, Isha had done a slow but sure circling of the group, probably with the notion of running out the door and out of the building. But suddenly there was this police officer walking in, blocking the way. Quimby explained later that as he entered the room here was this very attractive woman, if he may say so, very stunning in fact, walking toward him with an engaging smile. It caught him off guard, yes sir, it definitely did.

The next thing Quimby knew this sexy little package had punched him amazingly hard in the stomach with her right hand, high up, in just the right place to knock the wind out of him, while her left hand went for his gun. Not expecting trouble in such elegant surroundings, and having had the most rudimentary of briefings about a standard, white-collar arrest, Quimby still had the leather keeper attached over the handle of his revolver, secured to the protruding steel pin. If not, it might have been a different story.

Becky, who was standing closest to Quimby, saw exactly what Isha was doing. Without hesitation Becky grabbed Isha in a headlock while she was still trying to unholster the revolver, and flung the smaller woman to the ground with all the frustration of a linebacker who finally has that pesky wide receiver in his mitts. Becky followed her down and sat on Isha's expensive chest. Isha was suddenly hysterical, screaming a tirade about the intrusion, about the stupid fucking cops who think they own the fucking city, about Becky the clueless bitch and Andy the pathetic, stupid asshole, and finally settling on Mitch, how Mitchell Thomas had been blackmailing her to help him with his vile schemes and how she had been held prisoner by him and how he forced her to have sex with him repeatedly until Mitch screamed "Shut up!" at the top of his lungs. Andy figured the residents might have heard that admonition from Mitch three floors down.

Listening to Isha's mad protestations, especially her immediate and also predictable efforts to throw Mitch under the bus, and taking a moment to grasp the extraordinary scene — the detectives, Quimby still trying to catch his breath, Becky's vicious tackle of Isha, Mitch's back firmly against the wall, finally, all set in the luxurious confines of a penthouse apartment on Central Park West — Andy couldn't contain himself. He laughed out loud. It wasn't laughter, actually. It was more like a couple of barks. The sound made Isha want to kill him with her bare hands. She twisted under Becky's weight with all her strength, screaming more obscenities, and nearly throwing Becky, who grabbed both her wrists and pinned them to the floor.

Captain Jason locked onto Isha's eyes and held his finger to his lips as he bent down, gently moving Becky aside. Then he took Isha's arm and slowly drew her to her feet. "I would be more than happy to hear anything you have to say, ma'am," Jason said in almost a whisper, "but first I have to say, Isha Mowbry, at 11:21 p.m. on November 18, 1990, I am arresting you for conspiracy to commit murder. I also need to tell you that you have the right to remain silent. Anything you say can and will be used against you in a court of law." Isha's eyes were wide with apprehension as this large man slowly and effortlessly pulled her to her feet with one hand. To Andy's astonishment, Isha remained silent as Quimby slipped handcuffs on her, a click tighter than necessary.

"May I have a moment with Mr. Thomas?" Andy asked Jason. The captain nodded. "Be brief." He looked at Baker, who went with them.

There was a study off the living room. The three men went in. Baker closed the door.

"What in the goddamn hell do you think you're doing, you . . ."

"Shut up," Andy said quietly. "Sit down." Baker helped Mitch lower himself into an armchair.

"It's nice to see you too, Mitch. This time you listen to me, because I have information you need to hear. First of all, I have learned you are not my father, a fact that has given me immense pleasure. To think I might have been infested with any of your disgusting genes has caused me many years of grief. The relief is tremendous.

"Second, I have some news you will enjoy. Deedee, my mother, your wife — your ticket to controlling Moss Optics as provided by my dearly beloved grandfather — had been diagnosed with cancer of the pancreas. Stage four. She had about three months to live. So you didn't really need to kill her. But I doubt a jury will take that into consideration."

"I did no such thing!"

"More news, not that it matters where you will be spending the next twenty or thirty years, or perhaps life, but Deedee, my mother, your wife, produced a new will before she died. In her own hand. It has been authenticated, declared valid. Of sound mind and all that. Everything has been left to me. As CEO and chairman of the board of Moss Optics, I have terminated your services. The contents of your office are being confiscated as we speak. The news will be in the morning papers.

"I can't prove what seem to have been your attempts on my own life. Sam is quite sure there has been more than one. Although I do have a bank envelope from Punta del Este full of fingerprints, some of which I'm sure will turn out to be Isha's. That, a bank employee's identification of Isha from her photograph, Isha's pres-

ence on the bank's CCTV, the testimony of a Punta
hood named Carlo Solatto about a meeting with Miss
Mowbry, and the matter of five thousand U.S. dollars
should be sufficient to put her away for a while. It will
be interesting to see if there were any equivalent money
transfers under your name about then. Maybe we could
get you and Isha adjoining cells.

"Then there are the two goofballs who paid a visit
to Becky and me when we were at Sam's camp. They got
injured pretty badly, not being used to country ways, and
they are quite willing to talk about the nature of the mission they were on, and who sent them."

Mitch, who had remained silent, rose to his feet.
Detective Baker moved toward him, but Andy put out a
hand. "Look," Mitch said, his face a mask of truth-be-told,
charming Mitch at his most appealing, "you're barking up
the wrong tree. Isha has masterminded this whole takeover from the outset."

"Takeover?"

"Yes. Of course! A takeover. It's complicated . . . "

"I'm sure."

" . . . how she came on to me. Talk about blackmail,
that's her game, and she's a master at it. She's got the right
equipment for it, I have to say. I did a tight little stock deal
a few years ago. Not illegal of course, but a tad messy. She
found out about it, threatened to use it. She had me, then
unfolded her little plan for me to, well, you know, here
we are. She is so clever, so deceitful. Too late I had her
investigated. Some dark career she's got."

"You know, Mitch, I could actually believe you. I
could. But no jury in the world is going to buy it. You've

heard of smoking guns? Well, Mitch, we've got several of them with your prints all over them."

Mitch suddenly snarled. "You rotten little prick. For years I tried to get rid of your spoiled ass. You're goddamn right I did, you mommy's boy, always bailed out by that sorry excuse for a mother, but you always lucked out. That day in the tunnel . . . and you had to take a shortcut. Even RD couldn't get rid of you on the boat, dumb goddamn bad luck. You crummy little bastard." Mitch suddenly aimed a kick at Andy's crotch. On guard, Andy spun away, taking the blow on the outside of his hip. Baker grabbed Mitch.

"Detective," Andy said, "I think it's raining. Could you have a look?"

Baker turned toward the window.

Andy drove his fist straight from his shoulder with all he had. He could hear Mitch's nose break on contact. Mitch fell back into the chair, clutching his face, blood flowing.

"Oh yeah," Andy said, "almost forgot. George Cooper. Remember George, the guy you conspired with to wreck Mountain View? The guy who walked with a hefty six figures? We found him. I'm told he's quite ready to cooperate."

Andy turned on his heel and left the room, closing the door behind him.

Quimby and Jones had left with Isha. Jason and Becky were seated, talking. Jason looked up as Andy closed the door. "I was just finding out where Miss Cotton got her martial-arts training. All okay?"

"Yeah," Andy said. "'Dad' got a little emotional at some of the news I told him and did a faceplant. He'll be okay."

Jason cracked the slightest smile. "Good," he said, getting up. "Guess we're done here."

XXI

SAILING

Becky and Andy got out of a taxi at the boatyard in Fremantle around noon. It was a gorgeous summer's day, with the temperature in the low eighties. The first thing Andy noticed was the absence of *All American*. The rest of the competing yachts were loosely grouped on the hard, in the travel-lift area designated for them. Lots of work was going on. Each crew had created a semi-private base by the strategic placement of containers full of gear, or that had been fitted out as workshops.

"Yo, Andy! Here!" It was Sargent hailing him from a nearby dock. *All American* was in the water. They walked over. The crew was on board getting the boat ready for an afternoon sail. "You normally show up for work at noon?" Sargent asked.

"Where I'm from it's yesterday," Andy said. "So I'd say I'm early."

"Well?" Sargent looked at him, then at Becky, back to him.

"Oh, right. Excuse me. Guys, this is Becky Cotton. I'd introduce you," Andy said to Becky, "but I've forgotten their names." One by one, the boys stepped up, introduced themselves, and shook Becky's hand. "There'll be a test," Joe Dugan, who was last up, said to Becky. "Care for a tour?" Becky and Dugan went below.

"Fast worker," Andy said, shrugging. "Dugan. Who knew?"

Not a minute later, Becky stuck her head up the companionway. She was aghast. "You all are sailing around the world . . . in this?! You must be crazy."

"That helps," Sargent said.

"It's quite comfortable," Andy said.

"And safe," Stu Samuels added. The crew chuckled.

"We're going out, have a look at the new main," Sargent said to Andy. "Coming?"

"Yeah, sure. Okay to bring Becky?"

Sargent looked at Becky, who had on shorts, deck shoes, and one of Andy's *All American* polo shirts. She had her hair pinned up. "Well I dunno," Sargent said. "That's breaking the rules. But if someone flies twenty hours to go for a sail, I guess we'd better break the rules. We've got some extra hats." He raised his voice a notch. "All right. Off we go."

"If you want to tow the little RIB," Andy said, "Becky can shoot some pictures of the sails."

"Good idea," Sargent said. Teddy Bosworth jumped

onto the dock and brought the RIB around, tied it to *All American*'s stern.

They had a pleasant sail in a moderate breeze. The new main looked good. Becky did her thing, running around in the rib and shooting sail shape with different trim combinations, and with several jibs. They were out until dusk.

Back at the dock, the crew readied the boat for getting hauled again the next day. There were still five days to the start, and a few jobs remained to be done on the bottom. Andy walked down the deck to where RD was securing the sail cover. "Roger," Andy said, "I need a word." Davis stepped back, joined Andy next to the lifelines. He looked a little puzzled. Andy needed a "word?" Really?

"Mitch wanted me to tell you he's disappointed in you," Andy said to RD. "Here's some advice. When you want to get rid of someone, just fucking do it." With that he hit Davis hard with open hands to the shoulders. Davis, totally unsuspecting, went over the side. Andy stared down at the disturbance where Davis had gone into the water. Davis surfaced, and looked up at Andy. His face was blank. Davis held Andy's eyes for a long moment before he turned and swam slowly away.

The crew was mesmerized, staring at Andy in disbelief.

"Okay guys," Sargent said. "Gather round. Let me fill you in. You all know Andy's mother passed away. There have been some other 'issues' having to do with our sponsor, Moss Optics. Mitchell Thomas is in jail for several reasons. The bottom line is that our Andy is now CEO and chairman of the board of Moss. That means he owns, among other things, this boat. That also means he, Andy, is our sponsor. As such, and because of another issue, he has the right to fire RD — or any one of us nutty bastards he wants to get rid of. As you can see, he has his own way of doing that. Any questions? No, just kidding. No questions. But just to be clear" — Sargent looked at Andy — "I am still the skipper of this here boat."

"Yes you are," Andy said. "Mitch got one thing right. And there's no one else I need to fire. We are here right now on this boat in Fremantle, Western Australia, because a couple years ago at a regatta dinner at the New York Yacht Club I got very drunk and basically said if Mitchell Thomas didn't enter an American boat in this race he was a chickenshit, or words to that effect. That was after our friend Koonce over on *Ram Bunctious* had done one of his patented standup 'gotcha!' routines at our table, one of those Kiwi-magic raps where he puts his foot on your neck while he's supposedly buying you a friendly beer. One result of that memorable moment was me being forced to be part of this crew. I hated that idea, hated it with a passion. I did everything in my power to get out of it. Everything I could think of. And I was pretty good at getting out of things back then. But I failed. I was pissed. You know how I was at the beginning. You guys resented me as much as I hated being here. Andy the meal ticket. Now, I plan to do everything in my power to win this race. There's nothing I want to do more than buy Captain Koonce a friendly beer while I have my foot on his neck.

"Just to relieve any anxiety you might have, Becky will not be replacing RD on the next leg. She's very capable, but she doesn't care for the accommodations. Dick Hooper, who's been with us as an alternate from the beginning, will join us. He'll handle Davis's duties. Like RD, Dick knows quite a bit about women in addition to sails. He's arriving tomorrow.

"My only request, given the new order of things, is that we try to have more fun. We definitely want to win this thing. That's a priority. But so is having fun. We're sailing. Sailing is fun. We're lucky bastards, sailing the world's oceans with a bunch of cool mates. And getting paid to do it. Here we are in Freo. In a few weeks we'll be in Auckland. On we go, around Cape Horn. Is there a better way to see the world?

"In the interest of fun, I hope everyone can make dinner over at the compound. First, we've got this case of rum we need to dispose of. It's much too heavy to bring on board. Manuka Restaurant, Fremantle's best, is closed tonight, so they are sending a crew over to cook for us. Should be good. You got any friends, bring 'em, but tell them to hurry up because it is happening. Dinner is served."

"What about Willie and the shore crew?" Richard Crouse asked.

"Done," Sargent said.

There were twenty-five at dinner, including several women some of the boys had made friends with during the ten days they had been in Fremantle. Willie, his shore crew, and several of the sailors had set up a tight circle of tables in the compound, where there was plenty of room with the boat being in the water. The Manuka staff provided candles with hurricane shades, and brought a delicious sampling from their wood-fired restaurant that included a spread of bone-marrow butter with black garlic for their homemade flatbread, eggplant baba ghanoush, slow-roasted lamb, and a confit of duck rolls with sweet potatoes. The chefs grilled sirloin steaks, serving them with smoked butter and horseradish. The feast was finished off with dark-chocolate parfaits topped with baked meringue.

It was a balmy night. The temperature was in the high seventies. The wind had dropped to a light breeze, and the quarter moon was bright with a thousand southern stars shining in a cloudless sky. The candlelit tables, the rum, the amazing food, the full-bodied Shiraz from the Barossa Valley, and the moonlight had turned the stark, workaday clutter of the compound into a movie set.

"Race?" Stu Samuels muttered to no one in particular as he contemplated a spoonful of the parfait. "What race?"

The group had turned quiet after dinner, enjoying the moment. Eric Menici, BN, stood and tapped on his glass. "I just wanna say in case you all hadn't noticed, this is perfect. Look at us. Look at this." He gave a sweep of his free arm, a gesture grand enough to include the compound, the city of Fremantle, the country of Australia, the moon and the stars. There was applause. "You don't encounter perfection that often in your life," BN said, "so I thought I'd better point out that we are in it right this freaking minute." More applause. "That's the first thing. I want to toast our new owner, our new sponsor, formerly just a driver, an overweight pain in the butt before that, whom we need to thank for this sensational dinner. Andy, you have in fact become our meal ticket." Applause and laughter. "And for our sensational boat, not to mention the cool strategy that gave us a win by just six freaking minutes here in Freo." Big applause and cheering. "I dunno what happened back home, but here's the thing, it doesn't matter. Because I think we have stepped in it big time." Big applause.

Andy stood up. "I'm glad you said it doesn't matter because you're right, it doesn't. What matters is that we are here right now in this moment, and like you say, I agree, it is pretty damn perfect. What matters is we have a good boat and a crew to match and we are ready for whatever awaits us over the next twenty thousand miles. It doesn't matter because it is coming out all right. It doesn't matter that Mitchell Thomas and Isha turned out to be bad actors. You remember Isha . . . " The crew groaned as one, then laughed. "It doesn't matter because they will get their just desserts. And I'll tell you one thing: it won't be dark-chocolate parfait topped with baked meringue." Big applause and more laughter.

"One more toast." It was Stu standing up. "A toast to Becky, because I have a strong suspicion that Becky matters."

Everyone stood up. "Becky matters," Stu said, raising his glass. "Becky matters," the boys chanted several times, before emptying their glasses. Becky was blushing. Andy took her hand. Becky kissed him on the cheek. More big applause and cheering echoed into the Australian night.

Startled out of a deep sleep, Andy grabbed the telephone on the fourth ring. He looked at his watch as he mumbled a hello. It was six thirty in the morning.

The voice on the phone asked if he was up yet.

"Sam! Of course I'm up. Just returned from the gym."

Sam laughed. "Hope I haven't called too early. It's eight thirty there, right?"

"You're only off by two hours."

"Sorry. I'm a little distracted. Finding a new windscreen for the boat is like the proverbial needle in a haystack. But I might be on the trail of one. Gonna cost a fortune."

"You should get that guy who broke it to pay for it."

"He'll pay all right. Listen, here's a piece of news: Isha has escaped."

"What??!!" Andy sat bolt upright. "For chrissakes, Sam, are you kidding?"

"Sorry. Classic screw-up. They were transferring her, stopped for gas. She had to pee. They took off the cuffs, guarded the door. Five minutes later they broke the door down. No Isha. How she managed to get out the very small window they still can't figure out. She must be part octopus. Anyway she was long gone."

Andy fell back on the pillow with a curse. Becky was awake.

"My dad?"

"Yeah."

"Andy?" Sam said.

"Yeah I'm here, just stunned. Bloody speechless."

"Rebecca there?"

"Who?"

"If she's not, you're dumber than I thought."

"Isha's escaped," Andy said to Becky, handing her the phone. He got up, went into the bathroom. When he returned, Becky was hanging up. He flopped on the bed. The two of them stared at the ceiling.

"He's all over that windscreen. I knew he'd be pissed."

"Isha," Andy said.

"Should we be worried?"

"Maybe you should. You're the one who took her down for the count in the flyweight division. Me, naw."

Becky laughed. "That surprised even me."

"No worries about Isha. You saw how fast she threw Mitch under the bus. She wants as far away from this scene as possible. She'll resurface somewhere with a whole new schtick, hair to toenails; new name, new game. But it is goddamn infuriating. The oldest trick in the book. Leave it to Isha. Damn.

"But here's the thing. Isha doesn't matter. Like Stu and the boys said last night, Becky matters."

Becky rolled toward Andy. "I should show you how I took that bad little girl down. First, I got her around the neck, like this . . . "

Some time later, Andy regained consciousness. "I've been dreaming about Mountain View," he said to Becky.

"Really?"

"Yeah, I want to do it. I love this idea. We'd made quite a lot of progress. We had land picked out in Western Massachusetts for a nice campus, and some great drawings. I'll have to show you. It's a very cool campus, very outer-spacial, all round corners on the buildings like in those sci-fi movies, a little spooky, with this great grand-daddy of a telescope at the center. Everything is themed around outer space and the universe. Lots of technology involved. And some great little details, like the airlock sounds when doors are opened and shut. Even the drinks at the bar have planetary names."

"Tacky."

"Yeah, okay, it's a little tacky, but people love that stuff, and it doesn't take away from the legitimate scientific core of the place, the fabulous telescope every patron gets to use, the astronomers who will be there running it twenty-four seven. And the timing is right. People are going nuts thinking about Mars. The fascination with outer space is huge. I'm thinking we can get George back on board to manage the development."

"George?!" Becky said with alarm. "Isha's friend George Cooper who worked with Mitch to ruin you? George, who disappeared with the money?"

"The very same George, yep."

"Why on earth . . . "

"George has a degree in planetary science. And he was totally into Mountain View. He seemed really decent. He had good ideas, enthusiasm, good connections. He believed in the idea. I think we'll find out Mitch tripped him up, sucked him in somehow. And, of course, Isha reduced him to silly putty. That's a mistake anyone could have made."

"Ah-huh."

Andy laughed. "George has got some hefty jail time coming. Get that forgiven, put him on probation, and you'd have one dedicated lieutenant. He has a wife and kids. We'll see. I'll have a chat with George."

"You know," Becky said, "I think you'll do the right thing. But I'd keep one of those bracelets on his leg and a tap on his phone."

Two days later the Fremantle docks were jammed with people come to see the boats off on their 5,500-mile jaunt to Auckland, New Zealand. Jan and Andy had just finished doing interviews when Becky jumped on board. She'd been busy photographing the animated scene of boats, crews, and people. She indicated three crewmen from other boats talking with a tall, older man with a short beard and a head of curly gray hair. In his mid-sixties, he was fit, with broad shoulders under a light shirt.

"You'll never guess who that is," Becky said.

"Who," Andy said. "The older guy?"

"Yes. Grady Smith."

Andy was blank for a second, then stunned, momentarily stuck in place, reaching for comprehension. Then he got off the boat and walked down the dock, joining the sailors talking to Smith. It was boat talk, this heads'l, this tactic, that wind shift. Andy didn't even hear it. He focused on Smith, waiting for eye contact. When it came he stuck out his hand. "I'm Andy Moss."

"I know," Smith said with the trace of a smile, taking Andy's hand in one calloused enough to betray a sailor's existence, his soft blue eyes holding Andy's. Andy was flummoxed. What do you say to a person you've never met who you've recently discovered is your father? How are you? Happy to meet you? Where do you live? Want to get a coffee? Where have you been all my life?

"Good call you made on the way in," Smith said. "Well done."

"Thanks," Andy said, feeling a sudden surge of emotion followed by a flash of panic that tears were about to run down his face. He ground his teeth and thought about bluefishing off the coast of New Jersey, wet sanding the bottom. Grady Smith in the flesh, my father, a cool dude by the looks, hard to believe, my goddamn father! What a massive improvement, Andy thought. He wanted to jump on Grady Smith, hug him half to death, yell to everyone on the docks this accomplished sailor that everyone seems to know and respect is my father!

"Stay off the beach after you turn left," Smith said, talking about the next leg. "You don't want to be caught in there."

"Thanks." Andy felt ridiculous. "Thanks" was all he could come up with? After nearly thirty years, "thanks" was all he could manage to say to his father, for chrissakes . . . Then again, thanks wasn't so far off the mark. Thanks indeed for being the one to help conceive me. At least that was his first impression.

"Yo!" It was Sargent, reeling in Andy. Time to cast off.

Andy gave Sargent a wave, then turned back to Smith, who was already greeting another friend. "Excuse me, you going to be in Auckland, because we should grab a coffee, or a beer or something."

"I hope so. I'd like that."

"Great."

"Sail fast."

Andy met Becky halfway back to the boat and gave her a hug. Sargent hollered at him again. He'd have to wait.

Bluefishing and wet sanding weren't working. A couple tears escaped. Grady Smith, Becky. Andy was quite overcome. He was glad he'd have a few weeks at sea to take full stock of his bounty of new riches.

"I love you," he told her.

"I love you," she said. "Please be careful."

It was one of those lovely nights at sea. The moon was half full. Its rise through a turbulent sea of ragged, fluffy clouds had been gorgeous, constantly changing dramatic visions of light and shadow, each one more captivating than the last. Now the moon was ten o'clock high, casting a silvery path on the waves for *All American* to follow. The wind was abeam at fifteen knots. The seas were moderate. The boat was dashing along at twelve knots, feeling light as a feather on the helm, the wake a pleasant whoosh of barely disturbed water. It reminded Andy of a cat purring.

Sargent was steering. Andy should have been below getting sleep, but he found it impossible to leave the compelling scene on deck. Sailing at night was always dramatic, the water seeming to slide by extra fast, the red glow of the instruments adding mystery to the solitude, to the plight of a tiny craft powered by the wind with its cargo of a dozen humans suspended miles off the bottom, and thousands of miles from the nearest land. But this night was remarkable. The boys on watch were struck silent by their remoteness; in awe of Mother Nature at her best.

The genoa winch gave several clicks. The trimmers were on the job.

"Just wanted to mention," Andy said to Jan Sargent, "if you have executive leanings, there'll always be a job for you at Moss."

"Thanks. It's true, I'm not getting any younger. That what you've got planned?"

"I find offices a bit confining."

"I'm afraid if my blue carpet wasn't moving, I wouldn't know what to do. And I've got this America's Cup thing coming up in two years. It's already a handful. Maybe you should get involved. I've decided not to drive the boat. Maybe you should give it a go."

"It's gonna be in J-class?"

"Yeah, hundred-thirty-footers, stripped out. Grand. Amazing things. Crew of thirty. Spinnakers are ten thousand square feet. And made for TV."

The two men fell quiet for many minutes. Jan was engrossed in the pleasure of the lively, satisfying performance of the boat he was steering, into the game, part of the boat, reducing helm movement to a minimum, giving the boat its head as much as possible. Beside him in the cockpit, Andy was alternately sensing and hearing the boat like it was a living thing and contemplating the heavens that were such a vital part of his life.

"Do you think," he asked Jan, "we are the only intelligent beings in the universe?"

"Do you think," Jan replied, "that what we are doing could be considered intelligent?"

THE END

Made in the USA
Middletown, DE
22 September 2021